Marheh of the Silberay No.8

Mentor on the Water Road

Book 2: Return to Clanning

by

Rosalind Kentwell

L'Optimisme

Melbourne, Australia

Marheh of the Silberay Series

Book 1. Water Road Apprentice

Book 2. Apprentice Still

Book 3. Apprentice in Clanning

Book 4. Water Road Challenge

Book 5. Water Road and River

Book 6. Harbour Master for the Water Road

Book 7. Mentor on the Water Road.
Book 1. Darkness over Deerford

Book 8. Mentor on the Water Road.
Book 2. Return to Clanning

DEDICATION

To the God who is source of life and ground of being.

ACKNOWLEDGMENTS

I gratefully acknowledge the help of Elwin and Dorothy who encourage me to read my work to them.

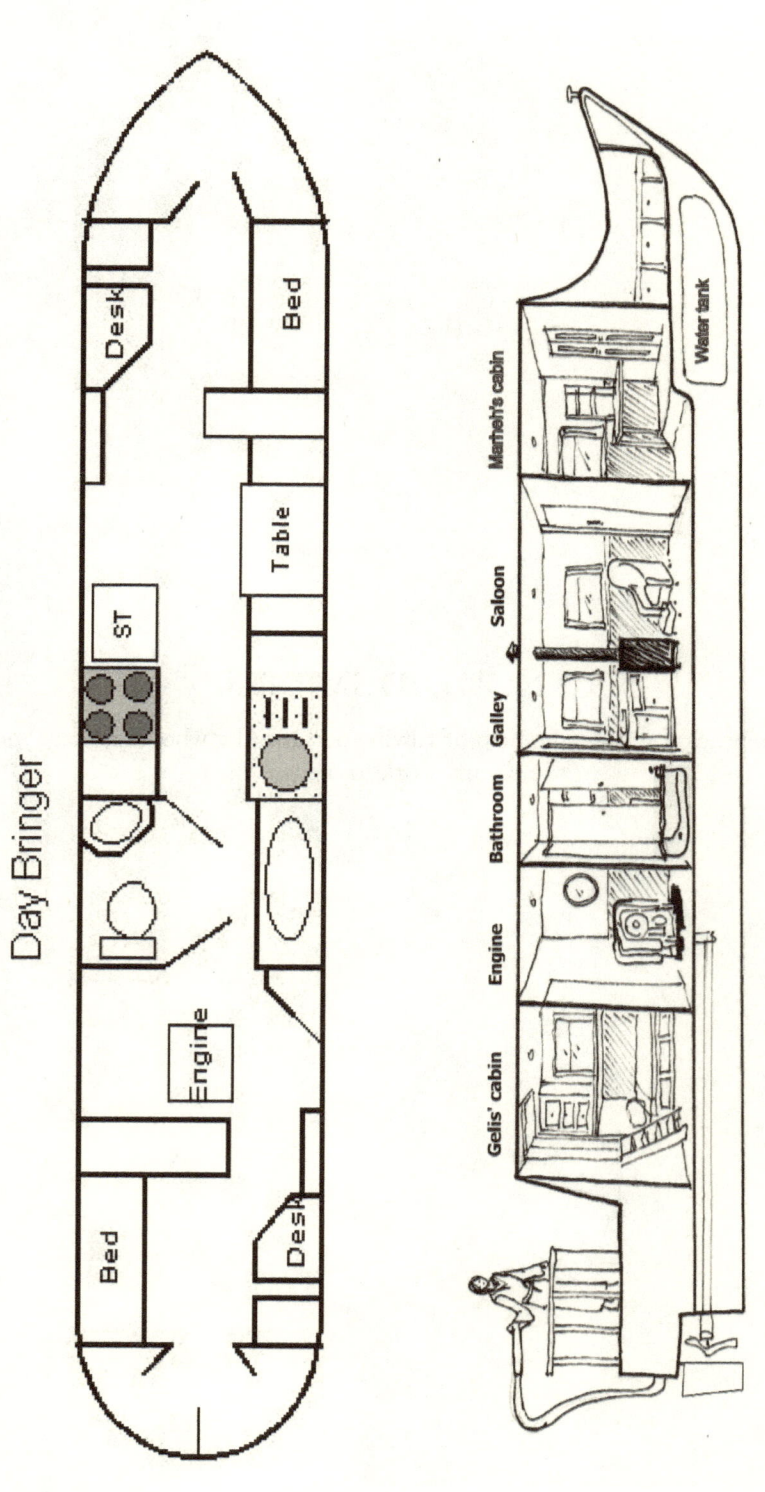

Day Bringer

Bed · Desk · Bed

Engine · ST · Table · Desk

Gelis' cabin · Engine · Bathroom · Galley · Saloon · Marheh's cabin

Water tank

Bigger Inside

CHAPTER ONE

"My apprentice," Marheh said affectionately. She held Gelis at arm's length, studying her and smiling. "A fine representative of the Silberay."

Gelis blushed, but there was no time to feel uncomfortable at this praise, too much was going on around her. Tith and Kina were saying goodbye. They wanted to go to their young daughter Nicken to reassure themselves that she was unharmed by her night in the YRTHA Clubhouse. Kina had a special hug for Gelis to thank her for her care of her.

Lorac, Marheh's great niece, her friend Ved, and Peter, the young waiter from the clubhouse, stood a little apart, wondering at the activity below them. They were not Silberay and could not see much of what was happening, only that part of the Yareblis marina that had been the village pond was visible to them, but there were Silberay appearing and disappearing from the water dimension and the sounds of voices in happy chatter.

It was a lovely morning, blue sky and sunshine to welcome those Silberay who had been imprisoned for so long. Marheh understood their mood of euphoria, but could not feel part of it. Perhaps she was still a bit disoriented after her battle with the Yareblis minds.

After they had retreated she had fallen into an exhausted sleep. It had been disconcerting to have woken and found herself in bright sunshine instead of the darkness of the boathouse. She had panicked for a few moments then remembered that Kel was there.

The adrenalin surge had roused her so that sleep was no longer possible but she lay for a few moments trying to make sense of what was happening, *Day Bringer* moving from darkness to light, the sound of voices, the shifting that signalled changes of weight, of people disembarking and embarking. Closing her eyes and hiding from it all had been tempting, but not possible. The thought of Kel had persuaded her to her feet and encouraged her out to the back deck to see who had taken charge of *Day Bringer*.

Kel had been there at the tiller. She had not expected the crowd of Silberay passengers but understood when he explained that he was taking them into the boathouse. Of course finding their boats had to be a priority. They would all feel safer then.

Since all the obvious identifying marks had been obliterated by the Yareblis the job was not straightforward, but the boats seemed to have an affinity for their owners. She stood with Kel while the others climbed off and scrambled amongst the boats.

"Don't you need to find *Storm Cloud*?" she asked.

"Loc will find her."

"I'm alright," she said.

"Are you?"

He took her in his arms as if to reassure himself of her physical presence. She let herself enjoy his closeness and care for a few moments then pushed back from him.

"I was so afraid for you," she said.

Her brown eyes studied him earnestly then she stretched up onto her toes and gently kissed his mouth.

"Go and find *Storm Cloud*," she said as he reached for her again. "Enough coddling. I'm fine."

She wasn't, not really, but the knowledge of it was enough to encourage her towards independence.

Kel studied her in his turn and she knew he had understood both the lie and her need to tell it. A moment later he had gone, leaving her the tiller and sidling along the gunnel until he could step onto another boat.

She watched him move easily from boat to boat, some now in the hands of their owners, others still awaiting discovery. Then she put a hand to the throttle and began to manoeuvre back out into the sunshine. The white boats were all gone. The Silberay were whole again. It was a start, even a victory of sorts, but not the end. The Yareblis had too much invested in this project to give up so easily.

Then she had seen Gelis standing with her family and someone else she knew. She moored and hurried up the slope towards them.

When the greetings were over and Tith and Kina had departed she sent Gelis down to *Day Bringer* to bring a stool for Bixa. Obviously none of them would be going anywhere yet.

"There were not as many as this at the Gathering," she commented.

"The Gathering has been and gone!" Bixa sounded surprised. "I suppose it must have if you have an apprentice. We were on our way back. There was no way to keep track of the days."

Marheh stretched out a hand to her but did not speak again until Gelis returned with *Day Bringer*'s two stools. She wanted to snap that she was not decrepit yet, but managed to restrain herself and found that she was, in fact, glad of the opportunity to sit. Then Gelis asked if she might take Ved and Lorac and show them where she had been working. Peter went with them and suddenly Marheh found herself as limp as a rag doll without her stuffing.

Tep sat on the grass beside the two women and for a while they were silent, watching the activity below them as the Silberay brought their boats out into the light.

"Tired, or worried?" Bixa asked gently when the uneasy silence continued.

Marheh looked at her then looked away.

"Both I suppose," she said at last. "Everyone looks so happy. How can I tell them that it isn't over yet? The Yareblis won't let go of this. None of them have been disabled. I don't know where to go from here and I don't know whether I have the strength for more."

Her words seemed to stay, hanging between them, and she wished she had not spoken.

"Of course we are happy," Bixa said carefully. "We are free again. There will be time to enjoy that before we understand the rest of it … and next time you won't be so alone."

Marheh was silent for some minutes then she leaned forward and gave Tep a little push.

"Come on little brother, tell me to snap out of it. I was just feeling sorry for myself. I wasn't alone this time."

Tep chuckled.

"Marheh the Great gone missing has she? You'll find her again – or she'll find you."

Bixa laughed too. Marheh released a long, sighing breath and the silence lost its heaviness and eased into peace.

About an hour later the four young people returned from their exploration. Kel had joined Marheh and Tep had left to go home to Fali.

"Gelis told us she cooked potatoes that were taken to the prisoners," Lorac said. "We thought maybe the Silberay wouldn't have food on their boats. There's lots of food here. We could cook up a party."

"What a good idea," Marheh said, looking from Bixa to Kel and back to Lorac. "There's plenty to celebrate, isn't there?"

After the young people had departed again Marheh sat with Bixa until Beuda, her apprentice, came up to greet them and tell Bixa she had found *Spring Song*. They all accompanied them down to the moorings. Bixa went off with Beuda to confirm for herself that *Spring Song* had taken no harm.

Marheh looked at Kel.

"Will you show me your prison?" she asked softly. "I want to understand."

The Silberay were mostly busy reclaiming their boats. No one paid any attention to Marheh and Kel as they wandered towards the patch of shrubbery that grew around the tumbledown shed concealing the entrance to the cavern in the hillside where the Silberay had been imprisoned.

Marheh stopped in front of the door, reached out to the handle and found it locked.

"There is a hole," Kel said. "I think Tep and Ved made it."

He moved to the side and held back the bushes that grew around the shed. The hole looked dark and ominous.

"Do you really want to go in?" Kel asked.

She studied his face, wanting to understand whether the place held too much pain. He gave a brief smile and shook his head.

"I just think I should," she said. "I can't experience what you did, but perhaps I can share a little bit."

He nodded and touched her lightly so that she smiled and leaned against him for a moment before bending down to scramble through into the shadowy interior.

Kel came in after her and stood with her while she took in the untidy odds and ends of equipment that had been stored in the shed and then the open door to the tunnel leading into the hill.

"We might just make sure we can't be trapped in there," he said, holding her back as she went to enter the tunnel.

She nodded but did not speak and together they moved a battered wheelbarrow from the floor of the shed into the doorway. Kel picked up an old post and put it over his shoulder.

"There is another door ahead," he said.

Marheh looked at him with troubled eyes then reached to caress his cheek.

"Off we go," he said lightly.

She led the way along the short, curved passage, stopping again when they reached another open door.

This was the entrance to the cavern where the Silberay had been imprisoned. She stepped inside, looking around in wonder at the dimly lit space. Kel put down his post in the doorway and went to stand beside her. For a few moments she seemed oblivious then suddenly she turned and reached for him. There were tears streaming down her cheeks. He took her in his arms and held her close for a few minutes while she struggled to compose herself.

"Sorry," she said at last, pulling out her handkerchief, mopping at her eyes and blowing her nose.

He gave her another little squeeze and let her go. She began to wander around the cavern, touching the rocky outcrops, some of which held stalagmites, gazing up at the roof where the shadowy forms of stalactites hung down.

"You were all here," she said. "In the dark and cold. Some people must have been here for weeks."

Kel nodded.

"And they kept you controlled and gave you food, but why did they want you?"

Kel shook his head.

"Thanks to you we don't have to find out. You released our song."

"Not just me."

She kept turning and looking.

"This part must have been here for hundreds of years. I wonder how they found it. I would have played on top of it when I was a child."

She came back to him.

"We can give it to Deerford now. It's beautiful really, don't you think?"

Kel nodded.

"I glimpsed it, once a day when they brought the food. It was something to remember in the dark. It helped my song.

Marheh put her arms around him and he bent to kiss her.

Sometime later they remembered that they had responsibilities. Their apprentices might want to consult. Other Silberay might want answers. Marheh's family perhaps had questions. Taking hands they made their way back through the tunnel into the shed.

"It would be best to remove the doors altogether don't you think?" Marheh said as they negotiated the wheelbarrow. "That way it would be safe for people to come in and out and no one could get trapped."

"I can see you've got it all worked out," Kel teased.

She gave him a little push and scrambled through the hole into the sunlight.

* * * *

Dinner had been a grand celebration. Alone at last, in her cabin getting ready for bed, Marheh thought back over the event. Whatever came next they had needed to acknowledge and affirm that the Silberay and the village were free again.

At Bixa's suggestion, the four young people had commandeered Dom, a Silberay who earned his living cooking, and asked him to direct proceedings. Between them they had provided generously for the whole group. Not only that, but Gelis had insisted they invite Marheh's family, Beytha and Evelyn and Peter's parents. Marheh smiled a little as she remembered how persuasive Gelis had been. She would have invited the whole village if she could have. She had the right idea. She was lucky in her apprentice.

Then, when those whose beds were awaiting them in houses had departed, the Silberay sang together.

That had been the significant part of the day. The soul song had been healing, but also revealing. The melancholy song of the imprisoned souls had become a dance of joy, but its light had uncovered dark places that would need to be addressed.

She finished undressing, put out the light and went to open her curtains. It was a bit like being at the Gathering. There were lights shining from some of the boats and voices on the bank suggested that some of the Silberay were still celebrating. She didn't know whether Gelis was on board but she couldn't come to harm tonight. Tomorrow would be time enough for problems.

She got into bed, pulled the covers around her and closed her eyes. She had found Kel. He was here. Her mind reached out to him with an offering of love and gratitude. For a moment he touched her in return. Then she slept.

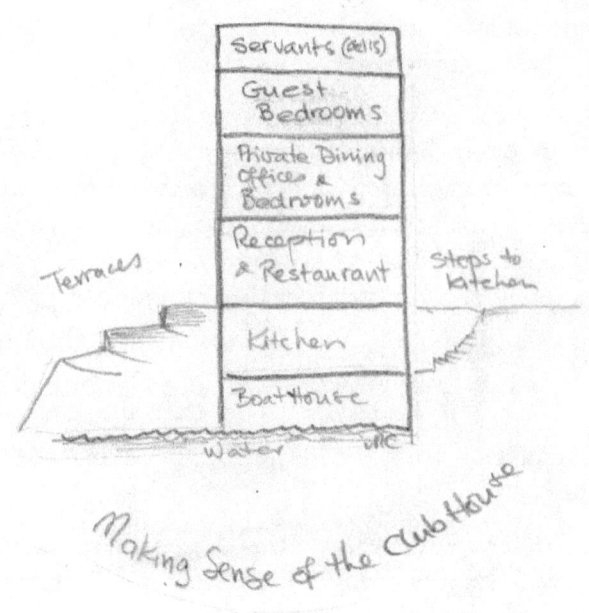

Servants (cells)
Guest Bedrooms
Private Dining Offices & Bedrooms
Reception & Restaurant
Terraces
Steps to Kitchen
Kitchen
Boat House
Water

Making Sense of the Club House

CHAPTER TWO

The sun woke her early as usual. She yawned and stretched and contemplated the day and realised that the weight of fear that had been pressing on her had lifted. Now she could contemplate another challenge without being overwhelmed. Get up, get dressed, there was work to do.

She made herself sperit and sat in the well deck to drink it, studying her surroundings as she did so. The grandiose club house towered above her. How had the Yareblis amassed enough money to build it? The Silberay were struggling just to maintain their Harbour, and it had been given to them. It was not just money though. The Yareblis were more interested in power. She still could not understand how they had been able to imprison the Silberay souls. She had always believed they denied the soul.

It was easier to see how they had managed to imprison their bodies. She had been prepared and supported when the battering began, the others had not. They shouldn't have been able to control

11

them though, not all of them, not strong, experienced people like Kel, Bixa and Chanra. They were mentors, but they had not been able to protect their apprentices.

Perhaps that was why they had been vulnerable, defence would have left them open. She knew, because she had made the same promise, that mentors vowed to defend their apprentices with their minds, or even their lives, if that was necessary. As a young woman she had cared for Silberay whose minds had been broken in the struggle. These Silberay had not been broken but controlled.

What plans had the Yareblis had for them? They could have broken their minds and turned them loose to wander helplessly without the wit even to feed themselves. Instead they had kept them, stockpiled them. The word, the idea, made her shiver. What had they hoped to gain?

She finished her sperit and stood up. Later she needed to talk with Kel and Bixa and the others and ask them what they had experienced, but now she would explore. Perhaps there would be hints somewhere in the clubhouse.

Leaving her empty mug in the well deck she set off up the hill, mounting the terraces until she reached the grand entrance that had so intimidated Gelis on her first visit.

At dinner last evening the Silberay had been happy to eat outdoors, sitting on the ground or at tables on the terraces below the clubhouse. She understood that. They would have had more than enough of confinement, away from the sky, not seeing the sun or the moon and stars in the darkness of their prison. Now though she would enter. She was going to look for the rooms Gelis had told her about, the private dining room, the offices, even the bedrooms.

The darkened glass of the series of doors gave back her reflection as she approached. It was disconcerting really, seeing so much of herself, and she paused for a moment to study the slim, plainly dressed figure she presented before stretching out a hand to push at one of the doors.

She needed to try a second and then a third time before she found one to admit her to the foyer.

For a few minutes she just stood, looking around curiously. The careful lighting, the impressive staircase all seemed designed to intimidate. Maybe she was foolish to be doing this on her own, but she was not going to turn back now and ask for company. The place was empty. She took a few steps forward, then a few more. Nothing else moved. No one emerged from a shadowy corner to challenge her. She reached the staircase, put one hand on the banister ready to mount, then yelped with surprise and shook her burnt fingers. A moment of thought and she recognised the illusion. Deliberately she took hold of the banister again, forcing her mind to recognise only the smooth polished wood. She was not often caught by a Yareblis illusion these days and this was not a particularly powerful one. She would need to be more careful if she explored further.

"Not if, when," she told herself and started up the stairs.

She found the private dining room at the top of the first flight. At least that was what she thought it to be. The long table with chairs around it could perhaps have belonged to a board room, but there was a serving hatch opposite the door and two elaborate sideboards, one on each wall. She walked in and stood looking around. What had Gelis told her about this floor?

A quick look in drawers and cupboards revealed only cutlery and crockery. The door next to the serving hatch swung open when she pushed it, but the little kitchenette was nothing more than it appeared. She stood for a few minutes letting her mind and heart listen but nothing spoke beyond an uncomfortable, prickly malaise.

Out in the lift foyer there were more doors to explore. One was open, as if the room had been vacated in a hurry. A desk and filing cabinets invited her attention. She opened drawers at random, sat at the desk and discovered writing materials and again set her mind to listen. Someone with more experience of offices would do better here than she could, but her listening revealed nothing new.

The next door she tried was locked. That would be the one to investigate then, if she could find the key. She was just wondering about the lift and whether to go up or down when she recognised Kel's mind seeking hers. She showed him where she was and tried not to react when he gave her to understand that she should not be exploring alone. He was suggesting breakfast and she realised she was hungry.

As she made her way down to meet him she tried to give unbiased consideration to his admonition. She knew he was concerned for her safety, but she was used to doing things alone. Of course that was because she usually was alone. Here there were people to call on had she thought about it in time.

"And if they had been awake," she said aloud.

"What was that?" Kel said, looking out of *Storm Cloud*'s front doors to greet her.

She stepped down into the well deck.

"I suppose," she said reflectively. "That since I am now the youngest mentor, I'll be expected to be seen and not heard."

Kel gave a shout of laughter.

"Fat chance!"

She raised her eyebrows and put her chin in the air then laughed with him.

"Breakfast is ready," Kel said. "Would your apprentice like to eat with us?"

"If she's awake," Marheh said. "She tends to be a bit of a night owl."

"Come on in. Loc can go and fetch her."

He drew her into his cabin and put his arms around her. She held him tightly and lifted her face for his kiss.

The sound of the kettle whistling reminded them that breakfast awaited. Kel ushered her through to the saloon and seated her at the little table. At his suggestion Loc went off to *Day Bringer* coming back with Gelis, looking a bit dishevelled and not quite awake.

Marheh smiled at her.

"Did you sleep well?"

She nodded, looking around at *Storm Cloud*'s saloon and giving Kel a shy smile.

It was not until their porridge had been eaten and mugs of sperit were refilled that Marheh raised the subject of their imprisonment.

"We have to know more and be prepared to defend ourselves again. There must have been fifteen or more Yareblis boats in here when I was drawn in. One way or another they'll be back. They've too much at stake to give up now."

She looked at Kel.

"What can you tell me about how you were taken? You're well defended. We've practised together enough for me to know that. You're strong, so is Bixa. Dom is too and Tippa but not strong enough this time."

Kel shook his head.

"Partly it was the surprise," he said slowly. "And I think there might have been an illusion involved. Loc and I were together on the back deck. I was steering. It was a pleasant day, no wind, so I didn't need to concentrate. Everything seemed as normal. I don't think either of us actually saw the gates or the Yareblis boats until the gates had closed behind us."

Marheh nodded.

"You think an illusion hid the trap?"

"I can't think what else it could have been, but I shouldn't have been taken in by it."

Marheh shook her head.

"You wouldn't have been if it had been the usual kind of thing. You saw through it once the threat emerged, but then it was too late."

"Then we were attacked and overwhelmed."

Marheh nodded again. She had experienced the attack and understood the strength of it.

"I don't know how we came to be in that cave where Gelis and Tep found us, but I keep remembering that time when you were controlled because they fed you some kind of mind altering drug."

He shook his head as if to rid himself of the memory.

"It all became a bit of a blur. I know there were already Silberay in the cave when I became aware of it. I'm not sure whether any were

15

imprisoned after us."

There was a short silence then Marheh reached for Kel's hand.

"You called me," she said softly.

"And you came," he said.

Another short silence then Marheh straightened and lifted her chin.

"We have to know more. There must be a reason why they went to the trouble of controlling everyone. Breaking your minds would have been easier."

She turned to Gelis, sitting beside Loc on a folding stool.

"You probably know the club rooms better than anyone else. Will you think about how we might best search them for information?"

Gelis looked startled and then a bit worried but she nodded slowly. Marheh smiled at her.

"We've been asking a lot of you I know."

She slid out from the table and stood looking at them.

"I'm going to find Bixa. She's the oldest one here. We need direction and she will be the best one to provide it."

Kel gave a little laugh.

"I dare say she will be able to curb your worst excesses."

Marheh drew herself up and her eyes flashed then she realised he was teasing her. She put her tongue out at him and whisked away, out through his cabin into the well deck and over the side.

The boats were not easy to identify in their grey overcoats. Marheh strode along the gantries trying to find *Spring Song*. She had almost given up when she spotted Beuda with bucket and scrubbing brush working on *Spring Song*'s roof. She remembered the year Beuda was apprenticed and what a difficult young woman she had been. Now she was nearly ready to graduate.

"Is it coming off?" she asked when she was near enough to speak without shouting.

"Fairly well. It's water based fortunately and more of a colour

16

wash than a paint."

She put down her brush and eased her shoulders.

"Are you wanting Bixa?"

"Only if you think she's fit for a visitor."

"She's resting in the saloon. I'm sure she'll be pleased to see you."

"How are you?"

"Glad to be doing something active. It was you who freed our song, wasn't it? Thank you."

"Not just me," Marheh said. "I'm glad to have found you."

She let herself into the back cabin and walked through to the saloon. Bixa sat comfortably in her armchair, her feet up on the footstool. She opened her eyes as Marheh approached.

"Marheh, welcome."

She held a hand out to her and took her feet off the stool.

"Sit. Will you have sperit?"

Marheh shook her head.

"I've not long had breakfast, but I'll make some for you if you'd like it."

"I'm fine."

She gestured again to the footstool and Marheh perched on the edge of it.

"How are you?" they said together, then smiled at each other.

They had known each other since Marheh was apprenticed, but only become friends the year Bixa became a mentor. Marheh had been standing in for the Harbour Master at the time and had asked Bixa's advice, since she had held the position for a number of years. That was eighteen years ago.

"You first," Marheh said. "How are you really?"

"Weaker than I would like," Bixa said, knowing Marheh wanted a truthful answer. "And not yet enough in control to practise the discipline of the mind, but very happy to be reunited with my song and be back on *Spring Song* and enjoying the sunlight."

She smiled at Marheh.

"And you? How are you? No prevaricating."

Marheh laughed briefly.

"No prevaricating," she agreed. "I'm fine really, but my mind took quite a beating and I know I'm not really fit again yet. Singing was draining too, but there are always rewards in the song however difficult."

Bixa nodded.

"And we're not done with the Yareblis, are we?"

"No."

It was a brief, almost curt response. Bixa stretched a hand out to touch her knee.

"How can I help?"

Marheh's eyes widened. She made a little sound, like a sigh, then found that she was crying. Angrily she rubbed at the tears that kept coming. Bixa's hand continued to rest gently on her knee.

"What an idiot I am," she said at last, fishing for her handkerchief. "Sorry to do that to you."

"Perhaps I should withdraw my offer of help if it has that effect on you," Bixa teased gently.

Marheh wiped her eyes, blew her nose and put away her handkerchief before responding.

"I was all set to have to persuade you. The others seem to be all celebrating, not many are even out scrubbing like Beuda. I suppose I can understand that really, but all the Yareblis boats have gone out onto the water road. They could have gone anywhere. They'll come back while they think we are still weak from the confrontation and we won't be ready."

"They will be weak too, don't forget."

"What I don't understand is what they planned to do with you all. Why keep you prisoners? Why waste strength controlling you when they could have just destroyed you minds?"

Bixa nodded.

"So what is it you want me to do?"

"Call a meeting. They'll listen to you. You're the senior mentor. We need to hear everyone's experience and try to make sense of how they managed to imprison you. I've talked with Kel, but perhaps it was not the same for everyone."

"We need to sing together too," Bixa said. "That will build some protection."

Marheh nodded.

"And I'm going to explore the building with Gelis. There is an office with a lot of paperwork, maybe Chanra could make sense of that, and a locked room it would be good to get into."

Bixa patted her knee.

"One step at a time. Give yourself a bit of space. I think we can afford to give people time to expand back into themselves. How about we plan for an early meal together and a meeting afterwards?"

Marheh nodded slowly. She couldn't help feeling that matters were more urgent than that, but she understood Bixa's reasoning and there were things she could do in the meantime.

The two women spoke together a bit longer before Marheh stood up to go. She could see that Bixa was tiring and urged her to rest. Bixa must be at least eighty eight, even a bit older perhaps. A word of farewell to Beuda, who was now scrubbing the side against the gantry, and she was off to look for *Autumn Wind*. Dom would be the best person to organise a shared meal. The Silberay were lucky to have someone with his skills and his willingness to use them.

She wondered whether there might be time to visit the pottery and check on the family but first a word to Chanra about the office and then she would look for Gelis and go with her, back into the club house to explore further.

Day Bringer's bright paint and shining brass made her stand out amongst the grey, but now there were colours emerging on other boats as the Silberay woke up and got to work. She found Gelis, rather damp and dishevelled, scrubbing alongside Loc.

"I'm afraid I'm going to steal your assistant," she told Loc.

He grinned at her.

"Oh well, it was good while it lasted."

Gelis put down her scrubbing brush and scrambled to her feet.

"I've been thinking about what you asked, " she said as they walked towards the club house. "There are places I haven't seen, but I think the rooms behind the private dining room might be a good place to start."

Marheh nodded.

"That was my impression. One of them is locked though. Have you any idea where there might be a key?"

Gelis thought for a few moments before replying.

"Not really, but I know a few places we could try."

She stopped as Marheh seemed to be heading for the main entrance.

"It will be easier to go this way, by the kitchen entrance," she said.

Marheh swung around to follow her.

"You know," she said, as they paused at the side door. "I'm really proud of my apprentice, proud and grateful."

Gelis flushed and turned to look at her.

"I wanted to help. I'm glad if I did."

She fumbled with the door knob, opened the door and led the way inside. Marheh stood for a minute contemplating the enormous white kitchen. Gelis waited quietly beside her.

"It must have been quite frightening, here, all by yourself."

"It was at first, but after a bit the job was so boring I had to remind myself about the danger – until they set me to look after Nicken."

Marheh smiled at her.

"I don't think any of her family can thank you enough for that.

Your note was very clever."

They moved together towards the lift and Gelis pressed the button to call it.

"This was just for staff. It only goes to the working places, except the boat house. Visitors had to take the stairs, at least I think so. I had to when I stayed overnight and when I was taken to the room where they had Nicken."

They stepped together into the lift as it opened.

"Which floor?" Gelis asked.

"Perhaps we could go to the top and work down," Marheh said after a moment of thought.

Gelis pressed the top button and they were whisked up to the foyer behind the private dining room.

"It seems odd to have a lift that only goes half way up," Marheh said as they stepped out. "This is where I found myself this morning."

The lift door slid silently closed behind them. She turned to look at Gelis.

"Wouldn't you think, if there are bedrooms, there would be a lift to take linen and maybe luggage up?"

Gelis nodded slowly.

"But I didn't see it."

Marheh stood thinking, then turned and pressed the call button.

"Hold the door for me," she said when the lift opened again.

Gelis watched curiously as she stepped back inside. For a few moments she seemed to turn inwards then she smiled.

"Come on, hop in," she invited Gelis and reached up to press the top button.

"But that wasn't there before," Gelis said as the door closed and they began to ascend.

"The Yareblis seem to be using illusions in new ways, to hide things that are real instead of making things seem real that are not.

Kel told me they hid the boats and the gates, that made me wonder."

A few moments later they had reached the top. The lift door opened onto a small drab foyer, lit only by a skylight. Gelis stepped out, but Marheh hesitated. If the Yareblis were consistently using illusion to hide things, then everything needed to be tested. Briefly she focused again then stretched out a hand to another button that had been revealed. Silently the back wall of the lift slid open to reveal a small, empty room.

Marheh, her mind still focused and testing, made a small sound, somewhere between a gasp and a sigh, at the pain and despair that flooded over her from the little space. Involuntarily she backed away from it, letting the lift door close. Gelis was looking at her anxiously and she hastened to reassure her.

"That is something we need to investigate, but not yet. We will need to be better prepared."

They looked around the little foyer. It was mostly doors, all closed. There was one on either side of the lift, one at one of the narrow ends and a whole wall of them opposite.

"One of us must be door keeper," Marheh said. "Not letting any door close until we know it will open from both sides."

Gelis nodded. Marheh walked across to the wall of doors and took hold of one of the handles.

"Let's start here," she said. "These feel fairly ordinary."

It opened easily to reveal a well stocked linen cupboard. Gelis opened the next one and soon all five doors stood open. They all appeared to be cupboards, the contents presenting a bland, unthreatening front, but Marheh was not taking anything at face value now. To Gelis, she seemed to be listening intently in front of each open door. The first three doors she closed after only a minute or two and Gelis understood these were just what they seemed. At the fourth door she stood longer then moved on to the fifth without closing it. However the fifth seemed to pose no problem and she closed that door too before moving back to stand in front of the fourth door again.

She beckoned to Gelis.

"Come and look with me," she said. "It will be good practice and you might be able to help identify what I'm seeing."

"I don't know how."

Marheh thought for a moment then stood behind Gelis, her hands on her shoulders.

"Try to put aside what you think you see and see what I describe."

Gelis nodded obediently. What Marheh was doing was a bit like talking someone into the water dimension and she had to trust her. She did of course.

"There are three shelves at the top about eighteen inches apart," Marheh began.

"I can see those," Gelis said.

"What do they have on them?" Marheh asked.

"Just linen, towels I think."

"Look again."

Gelis shook her head.

"Just towels."

What was Marheh doing, playing with her mind?

"That's what they want you to see. Look again. See if you can see a square box, a sort of crate, on the left side of the top shelf. Use your mind to focus, not just your eyes."

Gelis stared at the cupboard. If Marheh said there was a box then there was a box, but she couldn't see it. She closed her eyes and tried to picture the box then opened them again and for an instant glimpsed a big blue box that dissolved into towels again.

"Is it blue?" she asked.

"Yes."

"Can I touch?"

Marheh moved around beside her.

"We'll both touch. I'd like to lift it out if we can and see what is in it. There must be a reason why it is hidden."

As soon as Marheh's hand brushed over the box it became visible again. Gelis went to help her and together they lifted it out and put it on the floor. It seemed quite ordinary, just a big plastic crate with a white lid, but when Gelis started to pull at the lid Marheh stopped her.

"Listen to it first," she said.

"I can't hear anything."

"Listen for feelings, not sounds."

Gelis stared at her. Marheh touched her briefly.

"I'm sorry. I'm asking too much too soon."

She seemed to turn inward for a few moments then nodded.

"Of itself it can't hurt us."

Gelis pulled off the lid and they stared down into it.

"It looks like a big first aid kit," Gelis said, trying to make sense of the bottles and packets of this and that.

Marheh put the lid back and straightened.

"Somehow I don't think aid was what they had in mind."

The low light made it hard to tell but Gelis thought Marheh had paled, however her next words were ordinary enough.

"Help me put it back," she said. "I've seen enough for the moment."

Putting it back seemed to open Gelis' eyes to the rest of the contents but Marheh shut the cupboard door before she could identify many of the other objects. There were a couple more blue boxes and something slotted in upright below the top shelves that could perhaps have been a folding table. She couldn't help wondering why anyone would bother to hide the things. Surely the whole point of a first aid box was to have it handy in an emergency.

Marheh was heading for the door in the narrow end of the little foyer so Gelis followed. It opened onto a corridor that Gelis recognised. The bedroom she had been allocated the night she slept here was on this corridor.

"But I don't remember seeing a door here," she said.

Marheh showed her how it had been hidden by another illusion.

"But I don't think we need waste time out there," she said, allowing the door to close. "Their secrets are not likely to be in the public sections."

She turned back and stood looking at the two doors that flanked the lift.

"Which one?" she asked, but did not wait for Gelis to answer.

She grasped the knob on the right hand door, turned and pushed it open to reveal a surprisingly large, light space.

"Will you hold the door while I go in?"

Gelis nodded. She didn't need to enter to see most of what the room held.

"It reminds me of the science lab at school," she said.

"Science lab?"

"You know, where we had classes in chemistry and biology, only this is newer and has more equipment."

"No science classes when I was at school, but I left at fifteen to be apprenticed to my father."

Marheh spoke rather abruptly and Gelis had the sense that she was steeling herself for something.

"Stay there and don't let the door close whatever happens."

She took three careful steps into the room and stood looking around. Straight ahead two big sinks were set into a wide bench that ran the length of the wall. On her left, about one third of the way along the wall was a closed door and beyond it a large pin board. Pages with notes and diagrams were displayed, but she would need to move further into the centre of the room to make sense of them. Another bench ran along the wall on her right and above it were racks with what she recognised to be test tubes and shelves with bottles, all labelled, in print too small to read from where she stood. This bench had three metal sticks poking up, about nine inches high. The whole was lit by a long, narrow slit of window, high in the wall opposite.

She stepped further into the centre of the room then went across to the right hand bench to read labels that meant nothing to her and pull out drawers that held bits and pieces of apparatus whose purpose was obscure. When she could put it off no longer she turned to look at the pin board. The diagrams were rough and hand drawn for the most part, with scribbled notes and arrows indicating some unknown action or event. At the top of the board however were two printed diagrams, an outline of the human body and a cut away representation of a human head seen in profile.

Gelis, watching from the doorway, thought she looked like an animal scenting danger in that moment before the decision to fight or flee. But this was Marheh, she was never going to run away. She saw her step closer to the pin board and study the pages displayed there. Then she reached up to unpin two of the sheets and fold them, very deliberately, before putting them into a pocket.

That done she took a deep breath and moved towards Gelis. As she reached the door in the side wall she paused, reached for the handle then let her hand drop again. There was another moment of absolute stillness before she stepped briskly past Gelis and out into the foyer.

Gelis came out behind her and closed the door.

"What?" she asked when Marheh just stood, breathing hard.

She shook her head and held up one hand. Gelis waited.

"There is so much pain," she said at last. "But I might have found a clue to their purpose."

She closed her eyes briefly then looked at Gelis.

"I'm afraid of what I might find behind the other door, but it would be silly not to look while we are here."

She seemed to gather strength as she spoke and started to move towards the door on the left of the lift.

"Perhaps I could look," Gelis suggested.

"We'll stand in the doorway together and see," Marheh said and reached for the handle.

Emptiness
It was
Quite shocking.

The sunshine revealed nothing
In room or crouching woman
But showed me the tears on my mentor's face.

Gelis

CHAPTER THREE

"Have you seen Marheh?" Dom asked.

"She and Gelis were off to explore the club house," Kel said. "Is there a problem?"

"There might be." Dom spoke slowly. "I was pottering in the kitchen, working out what we might eat this evening. I went up in the lift to look at the restaurant and on the way back I wasn't thinking. I pressed the wrong button and went down to the boathouse. There is still a boat there, a Silberay boat, grey painted like they all were. I'm afraid there might be someone missing."

Kel nodded slowly.

"It does look a bit like it," he said. "But why ask Marheh?"

"She was at the Gathering, the only one of us. She would know who was there."

Kel nodded.

"She would I expect, given there were so few, but why don't you and I go and check the boat. There must be something on board that would give us a clue."

A quick word of explanation to Loc and they set off together.

"There was definitely no one left in the cave where we were held, was there?"

Kel shook his head, knowing Dom was just thinking aloud.

They went in through the kitchen door and hurried across to the lift. A few moments later it was open in front of them. They stepped in and were whisked down to the boathouse. The boat was tied in the farthest corner, grey and shadowy, a ghost boat in the dim light. The two men looked at each other then set off along the edge of the wharf.

* * * *

Gelis held her breath as Marheh tried the door. Some of Marheh's anxiety had rubbed off on her. At first glance the room seemed empty, just another space like the one they had left, only here there were no fittings of any kind. The light from the high strip of window bounced off the bare white walls and the plain wooden floor. Marheh took a step into the room, looked to her left and gave a little mew of distress.

"What is it?" Gelis leaned in to follow her gaze and saw a woman sitting on the floor in the corner.

"Keep the door," Marheh said sharply when she heard Gelis move.

All her focus was on the woman. She moved slowly towards her, one hand outstretched, then crouched down beside her.

"Toula."

She touched the woman's hand gently.

"Toula."

The blank gaze did not alter. She took both the woman's hands in hers and searched her face for some minutes.

"Gelis," she said quietly, still focusing on the woman in front of her. "Please keep the door open. I'm going to bring Toula out now."

Slowly and quietly she rose to her feet drawing the woman with her.

"I need to enter your mind Toula. Will you give me permission?"

There was no answer. How could there be? Yet she had to ask, and had to act, since Toula could no longer act for herself. Still holding Toula's hands she backed towards the door allowing the other's faltering steps to set the pace, her mind giving the necessary

28

instruction.

Gelis had many questions she longed to ask, but one look at Marheh's concentrating face told her that this was not the time. What was she doing? How could she help her? Were those tears she could see on her face?

Once Marheh and Toula were out in the foyer Gelis called the lift and, when it came, stood against the door so that it could not close. It seemed the most useful thing she could do and she sensed Marheh's approval.

As soon as they were safely in she stepped in herself. The door closed immediately and the lift began to descend.

* * * *

Down in the boathouse Dom and Kel had reached the *Boat And* boarded her. The back cabin did not hold any obvious clues, but as soon as he saw the work space Dom knew to whom she belonged.

"It's *Dawn Music*," he said heavily. "But where is Toula?"

It was not a question Kel could answer.

"She only graduated last Gathering." Dom continued to talk as they made their way back to the lift. "She's well defended, but very gentle and not very experienced. Otka was her mentor."

Kel nodded.

"They didn't engage very often then."

He pressed the button to call the lift. It seemed slower than usual and he pressed it again.

"Not often, no. Otka was very careful, protected her, perhaps a bit too much."

A moment later the lift door opened. It was Gelis they saw first, her eyes wide with surprise as she recognised them. All Marheh's attention was given to Toula and she did not even turn until Dom was suddenly beside her calling her name.

"She can't answer you Dom. I'm afraid her mind might be broken, but there is something different I don't understand."

Marheh began to back out of the lift, still directing Toula's steps.

29

"Why are you here? I'm glad you are."

"Dom discovered that *Dawn Music* had been left behind when the rest of us were freed," Kel said. "Shall we take her there."

It was the logical thing to do. Just being on her boat would help her recovery if recovery was possible.

Dom would have run ahead to bring her closer, but Marheh thought the walking was stimulating some kind of response from Toula so they all continued slowly, like a guard of honour, while Marheh went backwards, still holding both of Toula's hands, still guiding from within her damaged mind.

It seemed to Gelis to take forever before Toula was on board *Dawn Music* and lying peacefully on her bunk. Marheh remained there with her in the back cabin. Kel started the engine and she and Dom released the mooring lines. Slowly they motored towards the exit and out into the sunny morning. Gelis, standing in the well deck, saw heads turn as the Silberay realised they were coming, then heard, or perhaps felt, the collective sigh of concern. By the time Kel had found a space to moor there were Silberay waiting to take the lines and wanting to know how else they could help and who it was they were helping.

When Marheh emerged from the back cabin there were perhaps fifteen Silberay standing silently around the boat. She looked at the concerned faces and spoke quietly.

"Will you sing for Toula, and for me, while I try to understand what has been done to her."

Without a word those gathered turned to move back to their boats. They would pass Marheh's request to those who had not heard and begin the music that was the core of the Silberay life.

Dom put his hand out to Gelis as she stood uncertainly in the well deck.

"Will you go back to *Day Bringer* and try to sing for Marheh. That will help her best just now."

Grateful for his thoughtfulness, Gelis nodded. To help Marheh was all she wanted to do.

From the earliest years of her apprenticeship Marheh had learned to enter the minds of Silberay who had been broken by the Yareblis and direct them in the tasks of everyday. She had also discovered that she could sing with them. She had gone each year, with her mentor Nemle, and helped at Haven Cottage where Gip and Dayah cared for those Silberay whose minds had been broken in the struggle.

She had been resentful of the discipline it involved at first, but soon began to understand that she was learning, not just about being a carer, but about the nature of mind and soul.

Haven Cottage was gone now. Gip and Dayah had aged and retired and no one had been found to take their place. As Silberay numbers dwindled there was less money to support the cottage as well as the Harbour and the couple of Silberay left at the cottage were transferred to the Harbour to be cared for with the old ones.

These few had gone now and no one else had been broken since. Marheh could not help wondering whether this meant that the Silberay had grown complacent, but that was a thought for another time. Now, all her attention must be for Toula. There were other Silberay who could enter another mind, but none who had her experience or ability. Their song would keep her safe, however, and meant that she could give herself entirely to the work of healing, if healing were possible.

Taking a cushion from the saloon, she settled herself on the floor beside Toula's bunk. She began to prepare herself by breathing slowly and deeply and, as her body calmed, bringing to mind all she knew of Toula. She was a musician, a violinist. From the earliest days of her apprenticeship she had been happy to entertain the Silberay at the Gathering whenever she was asked. She was quiet, perhaps even a bit shy, and gentle, not a fighter.

When she had built her focus Marheh slipped respectfully into Toula's mind. If there was to be any hope of healing she must first ease the pain, sharing it, taking as much as she could bear into herself. It was a slow process and needed courage. Absorbing some of the hurt enabled her to see more clearly into the mind that held hers. Here was something she had never before encountered.

Fifty years ago, with her mentor Nemle, she had learned to enter another mind. She had learned to recognise and remove a Yareblis control. With Nemle's permission, she had explored her mind to discover the shape of the water dimension and then learned to disable the Yareblis by removing this from their minds. In the years that followed she had been tested by many different encounters with the Yareblis and her ability had been honed and developed. Now, in Toula's mind, she encountered a darkness that hid something she could not make out. Both the darkness and the thing it hid were foreign, intruders, trespassers in the gentle order of Toula's mind, yet they were not what she recognised as a control.

Taking still more of Toula's pain made no difference to the remaining darkness and there came a point where she could bear no more without it inhibiting her attempts to understand what she was seeing. Somehow she must dispel the darkness in order to address the hidden intruder. Her song would bring light, but could she remain aware enough to comprehend what it revealed?

There was only one way to find out. Holding the pain outside herself, she reached for the candle flame that was her portal to the song. Almost immediately music surrounded her, held her, as she built her own melody, but there was no light except her own. Later she would need to consider this, but for now her task was to sing, to make music that would spin light, and more light, until she became light and her song would flood the dark.

Pain, dancing joy, bitter sorrow, elation and despair were all woven into the music that spilled into light and burned to illuminate Toula's mind. It would be too easy to flare up and become nothing but the surrounding song continued, grounding her, drawing her back from the agony and the ecstasy that threatened to consume her.

When she was again aware of Toula's mind she saw that the dark place had been burned away and now, revealed, was an ugly parasitic growth. She could see too, that the growth did not like the light. She had a sense of it cringing away, almost as if it was sentient, but she had no idea what it was, or what its purpose might be. Nothing good, she was sure of that. Supposing she touched it, would it adhere to her mind as it had to Toula's? There did not seem to be much more she could learn just by looking. The pain she had lifted from Toula was nagging at her, hindering her focus. It would build into something she could not bear unless, unless... could she perhaps use it, transmute it into a weapon against the parasite?

She was prepared for the making to hurt and it did, a sharp, jagged pain that almost overcame her, but when she held it, like a clean, bright sword, against the growth, she saw it shrivel, slowly at first, then, as she pursued it, faster and faster until it seemed to have gone. She continued to hold it, lifting it, using its brightness to illuminate Toula's mind. She still did not know the nature or purpose of the growth, but she began to see the possibility of Toula's recovery.

Carefully, taking the bright sword with her, she withdrew from Toula's mind. Beside her Toula stirred on her bunk. Marheh opened her eyes and struggled stiffly to her feet. One last task before she could rest. The bright sword she held would return to her as pain unless she destroyed it and she needed fire for that.

The fire on *Dawn Music* had long since gone out but there was fire on *Day Bringer*, not just fire, but the promise of solace and rest. Summoning the last of her strength she stumbled up the steps out of the back cabin and onto the gantry. The sun shone over the quiet harbour and *Day Bringer* gleamed more brightly than all the other boats. In a trance of weariness she made her way towards her, stumbled again as she stepped onto the back deck and clutched at the roof to stop herself from falling. The steps down to the back cabin looked impossible, but suddenly there was Gelis, reaching up to support her.

Together they staggered through to the saloon and the fire. Marheh opened the fire door and Gelis saw her thrust her hand in. The flames leapt up, blue and purple and green. Marheh closed the fire door and turned for a moment to smile at Gelis. It was a smile that held the memory of pain, the invitation to rejoice and a sweet humility that thanked Gelis for her presence and her aid. Then she disappeared into her cabin and closed the door.

Gelis stared after her for a minute or two, wondering what it was she had done that made her so weary. She had done her best to add her song to those of the other Silberay and felt for a time that she had succeeded in a small way. There had been something enriching about joining with so many singers, but she had not been able to sustain it. At least she had been here, a physical presence, to give Marheh her strength of body, such as it was.

She looked again at the fire, but the show of colour was over and it had resumed its customary soft reddish glow. What should she be doing now, she wondered, moving restlessly about the saloon. Marheh obviously did not want her at the moment, but there might be something she could do that would be a help later on. Perhaps, now that Marheh had done whatever it was that she did, the others might have finished singing, some of them at least. She went slowly through the boat to her cabin and then out onto the back deck, wanting someone to ask.

All was quiet. Some of the boats had begun to reveal their true colours but the afternoon sun showed up all the grey patches. *Storm Cloud* was moored just behind *Day Bringer* and she looked wistfully at her. Kel would know what Marheh would need, but perhaps he was busy singing still and she didn't want to interrupt. She stepped off onto the gantry and walked a couple of paces towards her then stopped. She was about to turn away when a dark head appeared in the rear hatchway. Loc smiled at her and beckoned. She went gratefully towards him.

"Come on down," he invited. "You'll be feeling a bit lost I expect."

"Just a bit. Marheh came back so tired and I don't know what to do for the best."

"Kel will know."

Loc ushered her through to the saloon where Kel was sitting. He looked quite tired too. Obviously real singing, the kind the mentors did, was exhausting. He smiled a welcome as Gelis entered.

"Are you alright?" he asked. "Not feeling too confused by all of this?"

Gelis smiled back.

"I am a bit, but it doesn't matter as long as I don't get in the way."

Loc indicated a seat at the table and sat down opposite her.

"You certainly haven't done that," Kel said.

"The reverse, I would say," Loc added.

"Marheh came back, and she's so tired, I don't know what to do for the best."

"Just let her sleep," Kel said. "That's what she will need most. She wears herself out doing the work she does, but perhaps we should be checking on Toula."

"What happened to her?" Gelis asked.

Kel shook his head.

"Marheh can best answer that, or Toula herself if Marheh has been able to heal her. The Yareblis have been experimenting with her mind in some way I think."

He turned to his apprentice.

"Perhaps you and Gelis might go and find Dom. He will want to care for Toula."

He levered himself out of the armchair and stretched.

"I might just go and check on Marheh."

* * * *

It was early evening before the Silberay had re-established a kind of normality and looked to follow Bixa's suggestion of a shared meal and a conference of sorts.

Dom had found Toula, very weak, but whole, and fed her broth and sperit before leaving her to sleep. Lorac and Ved had arrived in the late afternoon, anxious for Gelis and Marheh and been pressed into service with Gelis and Loc and two of the other younger apprentices, helping Dom with the evening meal. Kel thought Marheh would enjoy having her family around her and suggested Lorac use the telephone in the clubhouse to invite them. Then Gelis suggested, rather tentatively, that Peter and his parents might be invited, and Beytha and Evelyn, because she knew Marheh thought it was important for the village to be involved.

The meal was served in the clubhouse restaurant, where there was enough room for them all with a little bit of squeezing. Nicken, full of importance, sat between her parents, Tep and Fali were one side of Marheh, Kel and Bixa the other.

Marheh was still struggling to make sense of what she had found in Toula's mind, and her state of exhaustion was not helping. She was conscious that this gathering was her suggestion and that she would

35

be called on to explain her reasoning, but that too seemed now to elude her. All she was sure of was that the Yareblis were not finished with them. A small sigh escaped her. That was not something the Silberay would want to hear.

Kel turned to her and put a hand over hers. She grasped it gratefully for a moment or two then smiled to reassure him. There was time yet. She could finish her meal and pull herself together enough to deceive most of the Silberay into thinking she had recovered. Only those closest to her would recognise the pretence, but they were the ones who would support her anyway.

Soon enough her empty plate was cleared and a mug of sperit put in front of her. She realised then that it was Gelis who had been serving her and smiled her thanks. She heard Bixa call for attention and listened while she thanked Dom and the young people for the meal and welcomed her family and the other villagers. Then it was her turn to speak.

She struggled to her feet and stood for a moment looking over the assembly and trying to collect her thoughts. Some sort of polite digression, a gentle lead in to what she had to tell them was what she was looking for, but she could not find it.

"It is not finished," she said abruptly when the expectant silence had gone on too long. "We have won some respite that is all and now we need to use it well."

A moment of silence and then a rumble of sound greeted this announcement.

"I know it is not what you want to hear," she went on. "But think about it. Think how much has been invested in the building, in the traps and illusions that ensnared you all. Think about how the village has been wooed and controlled."

She sat down abruptly, suddenly despairing. They wouldn't listen to her. Why should they?

Then Bixa was speaking again.

"I think we all know that we have to thank Marheh and her apprentice and Marheh's family for our rescue. Perhaps, in the past, we have been a bit to ready to accept Marheh's gift and her generous use of her talent and leave too much to her. We can't keep doing that."

She paused and saw the Silberay react to her words.

"What are we supposed to do then?" someone called out.

Bixa looked sharply in the direction from which the words came but could not identify the speaker.

"What are we supposed to do?" she repeated. "The very best we can to live up to our calling."

She paused again, waiting while the Silberay considered her words.

"We none of us have Marheh's gifts, but we all have gifts of our own that we have cultivated as we have practised the disciplines. What is important now is that we work together to decide how best to proceed."

She looked towards Marheh as if to invite her to speak again, but Marheh could find nothing to say. Patches of sound began to emerge, voices, not raised but making comment to each other, small rumblings, not all positive. Marheh struggled to keep her face expressionless. Had she been too ready to use her talent when she could have encouraged others instead? Had she allowed the Silberay to become dependent?

She was beginning to blame herself for everything when Kel's hand reached for hers under the table and held it in a firm, reassuring clasp.

"Don't be ridiculous," he said quietly when she turned to him.

She was still looking at him when, from a table nearby, Beytha pushed back her chair and stood up.

"I belong in the village," she said, as faces turned towards her. "This is our fight too. I want to pledge myself to resist the power of the Yareblis with all that I am."

She continued to stand, a plump, elderly woman with a determined expression, her eyes challenging her audience.

A moment later Fali stood up.

"And so do I," she said bravely.

37

Then it was Tippa, then Dom and suddenly an avalanche, until all were standing except one.

Evelyn still sat, not really understanding what had happened around her. Marheh moved from her place and went towards her, heedless of the tears that had started at the sudden surge of support.

"Evelyn," she said gently. "I know you care about the village. Will you stand with us?"

Evelyn looked from side to side and down, anywhere but at Marheh.

"I know we haven't been friends in the past, but can you put that aside for the sake of the village. I'll try if you will."

She put out a hand, but still Evelyn would not look at her. Then, as if from nowhere, Ved appeared.

"The village needs you mother," he said.

He took her hand. Her face lit up.

"Of course it does," she said, letting him help her to her feet. She looked at Marheh then and smiled kindly.

"Your heart is in the right place even if you do see things that aren't there."

* * * *

Bixa said later that she thought it was to the eternal credit of the Silberay that no one laughed.

She and Marheh and Kel sat together on one of the terraces after the Silberay and most of the villagers had dispersed. Gelis and a few of the younger apprentices as well as Lorac, Ved and Peter, were clearing up in the restaurant but outside all was quiet. The night was clear and still, the sky glittering with stars.

"It still places the heaviest burden on you," Bixa said into the silence.

"Not really," Marheh replied. "Not when all the rest of you are working with the villagers to put things right and build defences to keep them that way."

She turned her head to Kel and he knew she smiled.

"And Kel will be with me, to anchor me and curb my worst excesses."

"What about your apprentices? I still think they should go with you."

"Not Gelis," Marheh said sharply. "What if I can't keep her safe? She doesn't know anything yet."

"But you've committed yourself to her," Bixa said gently. "And she to you. Hasn't she already helped you to find courage?"

Marheh pictured her apprentice cheerfully waiting on her that evening, saw her curls, her smile and the red slip of a dress she had been wearing.

"She's so young," she protested.

"As you were once," Bixa said. "Would you have wanted Nemle to leave you behind?"

"But…"

Marheh's protest lapsed into silence as she considered. She wanted to shout that this was different, that she didn't want the responsibility, but memories of Nemle and her own apprenticeship refused to allow it. She sighed, just loud enough for Bixa to understand her displeasure and turned to Kel, hoping for his support. Instead she found both her friends laughing at her.

Marheh the Great made a brief appearance before she managed to laugh with them.

"Just as well I have you two putting me in my place," she said with a grin. "If Gelis wants to come then she shall."

"Loc too," Kel added. "Then, if need be, they will have each other for support if their mentors turn nasty."

Another smile to acknowledge his comment and then they fell silent for a while, each with their own thoughts. Sometime later they saw figures leaving from the kitchen entrance below them and heard Gelis and Loc saying goodbye to Lorac, Ved and Peter.

"I think I had better go and find my bed," Bixa said. "Unless there is still something…?"

She looked at Marheh, aware that nothing had been said about Toula beyond the fact of her recovery. It had been enough for most of the Silberay, but Bixa was conscious that Marheh knew more, that she had experienced the pain and encountered the enemy in healing her. Bixa thought she was probably as close to Marheh as any of the Silberay except Kel, but there were still times when she seemed remote, distant in a way that set her apart to a kind of loneliness. It might ease her to speak now, but it had to be her choice.

Marheh sat very still, very upright, gazing out over the basin and the boats. Kel and Bixa exchanged glances but she was unaware. Bixa had almost made up her mind to go down to *Spring Song* when Marheh spoke quietly into the darkness.

"Harvesting," she said. "That's why they didn't break your minds. That's what they were trying with Toula."

"What do you mean?" Bixa asked when it seemed she had finished speaking.

"The diagrams I found, the notes and the object in Toula's mind. They were experimenting, trying to find a way to harvest Toula's skills. If they had succeeded with her they would have gone on to drain you all of everything your minds held. That's why they imprisoned you. That will still be part of their plan."

She thought to keep me safe below
And down I went, reluctantly,
Churning inside, it mattered so.
Let me help, not turn and flee.

I stood and thought, then paced the floor
Gearing myself for defiance.
Red faced and bold I returned to the door.
Now isn't the time for compliance.

The silence between us seemed so long
Until she smiled. Nothing then was wrong.

Gelis

CHAPTER FOUR

Next morning Marheh woke late, so late, in fact, that she was only roused when Gelis, looking a little worried, brought her a mug of sperit in bed. She yawned and stretched and smiled at her apprentice.

"You've slept a long time," Gelis said, sounding almost accusing.

"Slug-a-bed, that's me," Marheh agreed cheerfully.

Gelis smiled uncertainly at the unfamiliar expression.

"You're always up early," she said.

Marheh wriggled into a sitting position and held out her hands for the sperit.

"Thank you for this. Have you made yourself some?"

Gelis nodded.

"Why don't you bring it in here and sit on the end of the bed. There are things we need to talk about."

She was not away long, but there was just enough time for Marheh to marshal her thoughts.

"First of all," she began. "Thank you for all you've been doing, helping with the food, welcoming the villagers. The Silberay are lucky to have you."

Gelis flushed with pleasure and stared into her mug.

"I'm lucky too," she went on. "Now though…"

She paused and Gelis burst in before she could continue.

"You want to leave me behind, don't you? I was afraid that you would when I heard the plans that were made last night."

Marheh put down her sperit and pushed herself up to sit a bit higher.

"I did think about it," she said honestly. "I was afraid, I'm still afraid that I won't be able to protect you from danger, but Bixa and Kel have persuaded me that you must be given the choice."

"Then I'm coming," she said fiercely. "I know I can't do much, but I can make sperit and cook a bit so you can rest if you need to."

"I think you do a lot more than that." Marheh held out a hand to her. "You give me courage and hope for the future, but I want you to have a future."

"I'm coming," Gelis repeated. "When do we leave?"

"Not until after breakfast," Marheh said, teasing a little. "Not for a day or two I think," she went on more seriously. "There are preparations we need to make, things we might learn from here. Most importantly we need to discover, if we can, which way they went – through the tunnel or under the bridge."

Gelis nodded slowly.

"And that won't be easy unless we find someone who can see the water road."

"It's quite unusual for the Yareblis to use boats," Marheh continued. "I haven't experienced it since I was an apprentice. Their boats were canoes then. They couldn't live on them, but from the glimpses I got of the boats that were here, I think they could on those, for a time at least."

"I thought some were living in the club house," Gelis said. "But they could have been living on the boats."

"Or maintaining the boats, ready to be lived on, to be used against those of us who managed to avoid their trap."

"I was wondering," Gelis said. "You said Kel had been trapped by an illusion that the gates and the boats were not there. Why did we see them?"

Marheh nodded approvingly.

"I wondered that too. If you remember, I had been describing my memories of the pond and the entrance to the village. I think that might have prepared us to see what was really there."

She drank the last of her sperit and handed Gelis the mug.

"Now it's past time for me to be getting up. Will ten minutes be long enough for you to make breakfast?"

"I've had my breakfast already," Gelis said with a grin.

"Have you indeed! Oh well..." She sighed theatrically. "I suppose I will just have to go without."

A boiled egg and a plate of buttered toast cut into soldiers were ready for her when she appeared.

"Breakfast!" she said, a picture of surprise. "What a treasure you are!"

Gelis laughed.

"My mentor is very strict. I'm expected to do as I'm told."

"Quite right too."

* * * *

Not much later strategic planning was underway.

Bixa was in overall charge, with Beuda to do the running for her. Tippa and Mok, one of the younger Silberay, volunteered to go and moor by the pottery to watch the tunnel, Pon and Sampi would go out through the bridge to moor there. Deerford would be protected from both approaches.

Chanra was bringing her skills to analysing the ledgers and files they found in the club house and working out how to deploy Silberay and villagers to reopen the shop and the pub. The Mayor, Peter's father James, joined with Beytha to support these initiatives and would talk to the villagers about what was happening. Dom found an ally in Evelyn, who clearly enjoyed the importance of working in the big kitchen.

Marheh realised that Fali might have been in a position to catch a glimpse of the white boats if they had gone past the pottery. She went alone through the village, wanting to stretch her legs as well as to see the effect of the departure of the Yareblis. She was still unhappy about Gelis' choice, but was trying not to allow herself to be distracted by the worry of keeping her safe.

With the sensible part of herself she recognised that it was too soon for much change in the village so she was heartened to see the shop was open with Jul behind the counter. She went in for a quick word and found that two Silberay, Als and Hela, were assisting him.

Jul greeted her cheerfully.

"I've no idea if this is legal," he said. "But the village needs the shop, so here I am."

He turned to smile at a customer and Marheh lifted a hand in greeting and went on her way.

At the pottery she was welcomed with hugs and sperit and found her mood lifting even further. Tith and Lorac went back to work after they had greeted her and Nicken was at school, but Fali, Tep and Kina remained in the kitchen. Marheh looked around at them.

"I'm so grateful for you all," she said, aware anew of their loving support.

Fali gave her sperit and another hug. Tep pushed the plate of biscuits towards her. She grinned and helped herself.

"But I haven't come to be fed," she said. "I'm hoping Fali can help me."

"You know I will if I can."

"You were here when the Yareblis left," she explained. "Kel and I will be going after them, but at the moment we don't know which way they went. If they came this way you might have caught a glimpse of them, that's all. Their boats are white and look taller than *Day Bringer*, though I suppose they can't really be much taller or they couldn't get under the bridges."

Fali shook her head slowly. She remembered the day, sitting alone in the kitchen, holding the others in her heart, anxious for Nicken and for Marheh. Later, as the sky lightened, she had gone into the back garden, needing to do something active. Would she have been aware if a fleet of boats had gone past?

"I think I would have noticed something if they had come this way," she said at last.

* * * *

It was enough, Marheh thought, as she headed back to *Day Bringer*. She and Kel had reasoned that they would go south towards the junction with the Great Northern since that would give them more options and now Fali had reinforced that opinion. That made it unlikely that the pottery would be targeted again, but Kina particularly, had been pleased to learn that two Silberay boats would be coming to moor there.

The pub had not opened, she noticed, as she passed through the square again, but James Corcoran was standing outside it chatting with a middle aged couple as well as one or two of the pub's regulars. He greeted Marheh and beckoned her over.

"Tom and Alice Ladbroke," he said, introducing the couple. "This is Mary Carron. She has been largely responsible for routing the interlopers."

"You'll be Felicity Carron's sister-in-law then," the woman commented. "You're Silberay."

Marheh smiled and nodded as James continued.

"The Ladbrokes had the pub until twelve months ago. I'm hoping they will return."

"I don't know why we left really," Tom said. "We never intended to."

"There was pressure," Alice added.

"It were never so good after you went," one elderly bystander put in. "No interest in the beer and only fancy nosh. I would have stopped coming if there'd been anything else."

"Obviously the village needs you," Marheh said. "What good is a pub with only fancy nosh?" She grinned. "Not to mention bad beer."

Tom nodded.

"I reckon we'll be back. Mr Mayor here says he can get things sorted for us."

* * * *

Things were starting to come right for the village. Marheh strode down the hill towards the gates to the club house, propped open now so that people could enter and feel welcome. It made her next task more important than ever. The village as well as the Silberay were trusting her to make things safe for them. For a moment she felt the weight of responsibility. Her steps slowed. They were asking too much of her. Then she took a deep breath and walked on. It was no good complaining. It was her job and she had to accept it whatever the cost.

She discussed her findings with Kel and Bixa and agreed with them that Yarla, the present Harbour Master, should be alerted, just in case.

"We probably should have been in touch before this," Bixa said. "She will have been concerned."

"I think she will know on some level that you are free," Marheh said slowly. "But certainly now the Yareblis are moving south she should know."

"The Old Ones are a strong defence," Kel said. "My bet is that they will find somewhere to regroup and look to return here."

Marheh nodded, that was her thought too.

"We'd best be away after them soon then, before they have time to organise," she said.

When she was younger and less experienced in the ways of the Yareblis she might have relished the idea. Now she understood that the struggle might cost her everything. There was sorrow in the knowledge, but her feelings were irrelevant and must not be allowed to impede her action.

"Are there preparations you need to make?" Bixa asked carefully, understanding that the sympathy she would have liked to articulate would be counterproductive just now.

"*Storm Cloud* is almost free of the grey coating," Kel said. "We need water, stores, just the usual things, and we need your song."

Marheh stood up and gave Bixa a hug.

"We need to prepare our apprentices too," she said. "Gelis is helping Loc clean *Storm Cloud*. I think we should check on their progress and talk to them together."

* * * *

"Could we be away today?" she asked Kel as they walked together towards their boats.

"Is that what you want?" he asked. "Wouldn't it be better to have a good night's sleep and be away first thing in the morning?"

"Of course it would. It's just the waiting. You know what I'm like."

He smiled at her and nodded.

"First light tomorrow then," he said.

* * * *

First light was early, not quite five o'clock. Everything was still and quiet. The dawn chorus had barely begun when Marheh opened the doors to the well deck and looked out at the day. A little shiver of anticipation, the sense of her heart beating faster, and she stepped out and up onto the gantry. *Storm Cloud* was shifting a little at her mooring indicating movement within and a moment later Kel looked out.

"Ready?" he mouthed.

"Ready," she returned.

Gelis was awake and dressing, the engine checks were done. The engine came to life when she turned the key then settled into quiet throbbing. She stepped off to attend to the mooring lines. Behind her Kel was doing the same. Minutes later they were moving slowly between the rows of boats heading out onto the water road itself.

There was no one about. Goodbyes had been exchanged last evening, but as they passed heads popped out of doors to wave and wish them well. Then they were through the gates and on their way to the bridge.

Day Bringer's chimney had not yet been replaced so Marheh had no need to worry about getting through, although it did seem as if the clearance was better than before. She wondered about the water level and even considered the possibility that she had been the victim of an illusion as they came through the other way, but put the thought aside. It did not matter now.

Storm Cloud was just a boat length behind and she turned briefly to see her come through the bridge hole and smile at Kel before setting to her steering.

Only about an hour to the locks. She had told Gelis that she would work them herself. It was, inevitably a potential place of ambush and she did not want Gelis to appear. Gelis had protested, but seemed to understand when Marheh explained how her vulnerability could distract her in a situation of conflict. For the moment however, everything seemed quiet and peaceful in the morning stillness. When Gelis appeared with sperit for her she welcomed her with a smile and moved sideways to give her space to perch beside her.

"Am I forgiven?" she asked, when she had thanked her for the sperit and given her time to speak if she wanted.

Marheh felt as if she was being assessed as Gelis studied her.

"I'm just a trouble for you, aren't I?" she burst out at last.

Marheh looked at her gravely.

"No. I'm grateful for your company and your care, but if I have to engage with the enemy I will need to give my whole mind to it so you need to understand how to behave so that I can do that."

A few moments for consideration then Gelis sighed and nodded.

"I'll try."

Marheh put an arm around her and gave her a little squeeze.

"That's all I ask."

They fell silent then. Marheh had already explained the importance of listening with her heart and although Gelis had barely begun to grasp the possibilities of this practice she recognised that

Marheh valued even the small insights that she could share with her.

Being silent with Marheh in this way was a gentle gift and Gelis accepted it gratefully and tried to give in her turn. It was easy then to obey when Marheh requested her to go below and practise her soul song because they were about to reach the locks.

Storm Cloud was still just a boat length behind *Day Bringer*. Marheh was very conscious of Kel's loving support as the locks came into view. All looked quite as it should as far as she could tell from her position at the tiller. As she got closer however she saw that the lock had been used to go down since she and Gelis had come up not so very long ago on their approach to the village. The bottom gates had been left open and the lock was empty.

We were right to come this way, she thought, slowing *Day Bringer* and easing her in to the bank. She hesitated a moment, gathering herself, before stepping off with her centre line and letting *Day Bringer* drift towards the top gate.

She looped the line loosely around the lock beam and went to close the bottom gates, holding herself ready against the possibility of attack. The paddle was still up. She took her windlass to let it down, even more certain that it had been Yareblis using the lock. No Silberay would have left it in that state.

By the time she had made her way round to the other gate Kel had moored and come to help her. Loc was poised with his windlass waiting to open the top paddles but Kel crossed to meet her.

"We could work you all the way down if you like, but perhaps it would be better to stay close."

She nodded.

"Did you see how it was left? It must have been them."

They moved together back towards the top gate. Water was slowly filling the lock as Loc raised the paddle. Marheh smiled at him and tackled the paddle on her side. The water level rose then equalled. Marheh grabbed the centre line and eased *Day Bringer* into the lock as the two men opened the gate.

"It feels to me as if they plan to try something here," she said stepping on board. "But it won't be until we are both in one of the

49

short pounds."

They would have nowhere to go then, trapped between the locks, but wherever they were they couldn't escape, not really. She watched Kel and Loc as they raised the paddles at the bottom gates. *Day Bringer* sank quickly to the new level, the two men opened the gates and she was away almost before they had time to lower the paddles again.

What would be best to do? Normally in such a situation, she would go ahead to prepare the next lock, only a couple of hundred yards away, then leave *Day Bringer* loosely tied in the lock mouth and go back to help with *Storm Cloud*. Not that Kel really needed her help since he had Loc. Was she being over protective not letting Gelis help her? She knew Gelis was not happy with her decision.

Day Bringer was half way down the pound and she still had not made up her mind. She looked back. Kel waved to her.

"Stop dithering," she said aloud.

The sensible thing would be to continue and prepare the next lock to take advantage of the water that would soon be released from the last one.

She had not reached the lock when the door to the back cabin was pushed open. Gelis stood on the bottom step looking out at her.

"You let me choose to come," she said abruptly. "I might as well have chosen to stay if you won't let me help."

Marheh bit back her initial response and studied Gelis' face for a moment or two. She looked as if she had worked herself up to make her declaration, a bit flushed and very determined.

"You'd best come and take the tiller then," she said at last.

Gelis took a step up and then another, not quite certain. Marheh held out a hand.

"Come on. I won't bite. I'm sorry."

A smile, a couple of rapid steps and she had taken her place beside Marheh who gave her a little squeeze and indicated the tiller.

"Put me off here and hover for a bit. I'll go and set the lock. I know you want to, but I really want you to stay safe on *Day Bringer* …

please."

Gelis flushed and nodded. Marheh smiled at her and stepped off and went striding towards the lock.

This one too was empty and the bottom gates left open. It must have taken half a day to get all the white boats down the three locks. Obviously the last of them had just done the minimum. Where had they run to? She went about the necessary tasks with only half her mind on the job. The other half was waiting, alert for the attack she had been sure would come here at the locks.

Day Bringer went down without incident and Gelis moved her very slowly onward while Marheh remained to set the lock filling again for Kel. That done, she set off, jogging easily, for the last lock.

She had just about drawn level with *Day Bringer* when she heard Gelis cry out and saw her duck. Then she ducked again, covering her head with one arm. She obviously felt herself under threat but was still managing to hold onto the tiller.

"Look hard," Marheh sent to her mind. "Remember the tunnel."

She picked up her pace to catch up with *Day Bringer*, pass her, so she could turn back to look at Gelis, who was still frantically trying to avoid the illusion that was bombarding her without letting go of the tiller.

She sent her warmth and reassurance, praising her courage and urging her to look and see. All her attention was given to Gelis so that the three figures that sprang up from below the lock were upon her before she knew it.

A shout from Loc, waiting with his windlass above her, alerted her in time to avoid the one with the club that was raised to strike, but the other two had tackled her to the ground before she could refocus her mind to stop them. A minute of breathless struggle, the sound of feet pounding towards her and then she managed to act, stopping first one and then the other before the third ran from the threat of Loc's approach.

She was still on the ground beneath one of the men she had controlled when Loc arrived beside her closely followed by Kel. She managed to turn her head and smile as he plopped down beside her then he and Loc together lifted the man enough for her to wriggle out from under him. Kel helped her to her feet and held her for a few moments. They were both breathing hard. Marheh tilted her head to look at him.

"We must be getting old," she said lightly.

Kel tightened his hold for a moment then let her go.

Immediately she turned to look to Gelis, but she was calm now, still standing at the tiller. *Day Bringer* was in the lock mouth going nowhere, which gave her space to look back to Marheh who waved and called to reassure her. Then she turned back to look at the two men she had controlled.

"Are they Yareblis?" Loc asked.

"I think they must be. It isn't typical Yareblis behaviour, usually they recruit others for a physical attack, but here on the edge of the water road they couldn't be sure others would see me."

She might have continued to cogitate, but Gelis shouted suddenly. They all looked towards her and saw a white boat fleeing along the water road below the lock.

"Definitely Yareblis then," Kel said. He turned to his apprentice. "Will you go and work the lock for Gelis while Marheh and I take care of these two?"

"Stay with her till I come," Marheh added. "An illusion attacked her before the lock."

Before he had gone a dozen paces Marheh's attention was back with her captives. She and Kel had worked together to remove the water dimension from the minds of their enemies often enough that there was no need for words between them. Since she was already controlling them, she would maintain the control while Kel entered their minds and removed the shape that enabled them to see the water road. When they had done, the men would not know what they lacked. Their values would not have changed, but they would have lost the power to control.

This time it seemed sensible to wait to release them until they were both safely back on board. Kel hurried back to *Storm Cloud*, floating in the lock above, needing to be rid of the shapes he had excised. Burning them worked best and there was usually a fire going in the boats except in the height of summer.

Marheh followed more slowly, thinking to help work the lock since his apprentice was with Gelis. Kel was tired she knew. When she reached the lock side she looked back at the two men, one lying on the ground, the other on one knee. They could have chosen to become Silberay, she thought sadly. She slotted her windlass onto the paddle mechanism and waited, looking for Kel's signal. Once the water was behaving as it should she turned her attention to the two men, released them from her control then watched as they stood and looked around, as if puzzled, before making their way away across the field beside them.

It was not very long before *Storm Cloud* was through the last lock and moored up just ahead of *Day Bringer*. Gelis and Loc were there, ready to help if needed. Marheh thought perhaps they had been discussing their decrepit elders and hid a smile.

"We thought lunch might be a good idea, since we've stopped," Gelis said. "Loc and I have made sandwiches and the kettle is on."

"That was thoughtful," Marheh said.

Part of her wanted to keep after the enemy, but she and Kel were both tired now and the white *Boat A*lready out of sight. She grinned at Kel.

"Shall we let our apprentices look after us?"

"Why not?"

Lunch on *Day Bringer* was a good opportunity to take stock and discuss what had happened as well as what they should do next. Marheh had a word of praise for Gelis.

"You did well to manage *Day Bringer* and the illusion. Was it the bird again?"

Gelis nodded.

"But not as bad as in the tunnel and you helped."

"I'm glad. These illusions seem to be able to home in on our worst nightmares. With me it was the loss of my hands."

She gave a little shudder.

53

"The worst one made me believe that the mooring line had sliced my hands in half."

"Ugh, nasty," Loc said. "With me it is fire. I've a horror of burning."

Kel smiled at him.

"I was the same, still am really, I suppose, but one thing these illusions do for us is show us what we most fear. We can't pretend. We might still be afraid, but the fear loses much of its power over us once we recognise it."

A few moments of silence honoured these words before Marheh brought them back to considering their next steps.

"Not that there is really much choice," she said. "We go on. The difficulty will be to work out which way they turn at the junction."

Hidden Lookout

CHAPTER FIVE

They reached the junction with the Great Northern late in the evening of the following day. By the time they had moored there was not enough light left to reveal any physical signs of the Yareblis passing. There had been no further attacks either and Marheh could not shake off a sense of apprehension, a feeling that the next encounter would have far more weight behind it.

The four of them shared a late meal and arranged a roster for singing through the night. Neither Gelis nor Loc were experienced enough to sing alone in this situation but they would learn by offering their song, as best they could, to support Marheh and Kel.

Marheh would take the first watch. As soon as this was decided she left the others to do what ever clearing up was necessary and disappeared into her cabin.

Quietly, already preparing herself, she lit her candle and changed into her night clothes. This singing would push against the darkness, a voyage of discovery to which she would give herself totally. She would sleep afterwards and her rest would be more refreshing if she was comfortable.

She lay on her bed on her back and spent a moment enjoying the candlelight as it flickered and danced on the walls of her cabin. Then her portal beckoned and she was away. Her song swelled within her. As it grew she encountered other voices, some that held themselves ready to provide harmony for her melody, others whose melodies danced contrapuntally around her. Her song greeted them all, acknowledging their gift of music, of support, but soon enough she pushed outward, beyond them.

There was light where she had been and for a time its glow followed her, filtering into the darkness that began to weigh on her, threatening to extinguish both song and singer. Still she continued outward, her sweetest sounds braving the darkness, carrying light and love. There was pain in the giving and the struggle, but the melody grew ever sweeter and more joyful as she sang and the darkness retreated a little with the brightness of it.

The entry of another singer drew her back in the end. This song called for her to complete it, a solid, trustworthy tune that she could rest on, acknowledge and give way to. Kel, she thought, sliding into sleep.

Next morning Gelis woke her, bearing a steaming mug of sperit and a worried expression.

"What's the matter?"

Marheh yawned and stretched and saw the bright morning.

"On dear, is that the time? I have slept late."

"You never sleep late and that's twice now."

Gelis sounded as if she was accusing her of something. Marheh smiled and pushed back the bed clothes.

"Any sign of life on *Storm Cloud*?"

Gelis shook her head.

"I've been awake for ages."

"It's the singing," Marheh said gently. "We might have overdone it, but it seemed important."

She took the mug that Gelis still held out to her and drank from it.

"I tried," Gelis said. "I think I heard the music, but I wasn't part of it."

"If you heard it you were part of it. Your song will happen. Does it feel to you as if we have made a difference to anything?"

Gelis looked startled for a moment and then thoughtful.

"I... I'm not sure, perhaps it is just the sunshine." She looked at Marheh. "The weight has lifted a bit."

Marheh smiled then drained her mug.

"Good." She handed the mug to Gelis. "Now, I've been lazy long enough, a shower and breakfast and we can be on our way."

By the time she was dressed Kel and Loc had joined Gelis in the saloon, bringing a pan of scrambled eggs to add to the toast Gelis had made.

"Now," Kel said when they had finished eating. "Which way?"

"South I think," Marheh said. "Unless there is evidence to show they've gone north."

"What kind of evidence?" Gelis asked.

"Damage to the banks, rubbish in the water, that sort of thing."

"Won't they have tried not to leave evidence?" Loc asked.

"They probably wouldn't consider that those things are evidence," Kel said. "The water road has never been part of their lives as it is of ours." He turned to Marheh. "Any particular reason why you say south?"

"That way is the Harbour, but more particularly that way is the Clanning Branch. I can't help remembering what happened to us there at the entrance. That was no illusion, there was real wire around the propeller and I'm still missing a shirt and trousers that dissolved in the water. I wouldn't be a bit surprised if they have holed up there." She thought for a minute. "The Clanning Branch itself looked impassable, but I was concentrating on the service area and then on the propeller. It is not beyond the bounds of possibility that they have created an illusion making it seem that way."

Kel nodded.

"That makes sense. All the same, Loc and I might just take a quick look in the other direction, just in case. The speed they were travelling was enough to create the sort of wash that could damage the bank. Loc, I'll put you off over on the tow path and back up a hundred yards or so. That should be enough for us to get an idea with two of us looking from different angles."

Marheh felt confident that she was correct in thinking that the Yareblis had turned to the south, but she saw the sense in Kel's suggestion. Speed was not so important now, better to be certain. She and Gelis took charge of the washing up and a few minutes later *Storm Cloud* moved slowly past them and into the Great Northern.

"Do you think we will find them?" Gelis asked as she scrubbed at the scrambled egg pan.

"If they are still on the water road we will."

Marheh was drying cutlery and feeding it into its place in the drawer.

"What...?"

"What will we do when we find them?"

Gelis nodded.

"It depends. I've got some ideas but..." She shrugged. "We'll have to see."

They finished the dishes in silence and made *Day Bringer* ready for departure. Marheh was at the tiller and Gelis on the bank with the centre line when Kel signalled.

"South," Marheh said as Gelis coiled the line and stepped on board.

They turned into the Great Northern just ahead of *Storm Cloud* and set off.

"It isn't very far to the Clanning Branch, is it?" Gelis said when she had seen Kel pick up Loc and fall in behind them.

"Half a day, perhaps a bit more if we go carefully."

Marheh seemed quiet and a bit abstracted for the first part of the journey. Gelis was careful not to tease her with questions, but she could not help feeling anxious about the coming encounter. What part could she play? Would Marheh allow her to take part at all?

Storm Cloud was only a couple of boat lengths behind them, which made her feel more confident. Loc had been kind and welcoming and she could see that Marheh relied on Kel.

They had been travelling for a couple of hours when Marheh's quiet mood changed. Gelis, watching her, thought she had finally come to some decision. She answered briskly when Gelis asked her what she had planned then handed over the tiller and asked to be put ashore.

"But don't go past me," she said as she stepped off onto the towpath. "Keep well back."

What are you going to do?"

"Reconnoitre."

She set off at a good pace. Gelis, following slowly on *Day Bringer*, watched as she strode ahead with seeming ease. *Storm Cloud* came closer and then edged up alongside so that Kel could shout a question, but Gelis could only give the answer that Marheh had given her. Then, as *Storm Cloud* was easing back again to give room for *Day Bringer* to pass under a bridge, they saw her leave the path and run lightly up to the crest of the arch.

The countryside around about was quite flat, but even so they were still too far from the Clanning Branch for there to be any kind of a view. What was she looking for?

She stood looking out until *Day Bringer* had almost entered the bridge hole then she ran down to be ready to step on board again as Gelis slowed for the narrow entrance to the bridge.

"I'm going down to look at the chart," she said, disappearing into the back cabin before Gelis could ask her what she had seen.

When she returned she sent Gelis to take the front line and signalled to *Storm Cloud* that she was about to moor. Five minutes later the two boats were secured neatly against the bank and Marheh was persuading Kel and Loc to join her and Gelis on *Day Bringer* so she could discuss her plan.

"It is not going to be possible to take the boats near enough without being seen," she began when they were all seated and supplied with sperit.

"I was not expecting to," Kel said.

"But if we want to disable as many as possible," she went on, barely acknowledging his remark. "Then one of us needs to be close enough to reach them. It can only be you or me and, since I'm better at it, I think it should be me."

Gelis thought she looked a bit defiant as she said this and understood that Kel was ready to protest.

"You are better at it," he said. "But why shouldn't we both go? Gelis and Loc are capable of minding the boats."

She shook her head.

"But not capable of receiving the water dimension when I've taken it. If I'm to be quick and accurate I'll need to be rid of what I've taken. If you are here I can send it to you to put on the fire."

Kel did not look convinced.

"You know it makes the best use of our skill."

She paused and looked at the two apprentices.

"And Loc and Gelis will be here to mind the boats and watch for trouble while we are otherwise occupied."

Gelis wondered if she looked as confused as she felt.

"I've looked at the chart," Marheh continued. "The Clanning Branch comes off the Great Northern at an angle, back this way. If we go on for another hour it will be near enough for me to walk across and get behind them, but our boats won't be close enough to alert them."

"I don't like it," Kel said. "You'll be too vulnerable once you start to act, and what if you're wrong about them being in the Clanning Branch, or if they have gone much further than the entrance?"

"Then I'll have had the walk for nothing, but at least we'll know."

There had nearly been an argument, Gelis thought, as she stood with the front line ready for Marheh's signal. Kel obviously thought that Marheh would be putting herself at risk and wanted to go with her, or at least send Loc with her to watch over her. Marheh said she would be better able to hide alone and didn't need anyone to protect her. She and Loc had kept silent. At last Marheh had called a halt by suggesting that they at least go along to the place she wanted them to moor. They could think about the pros and cons as they went.

Marheh was very quiet as they travelled along. It was not an easy silence either. Gelis looked at her from time to time with troubled eyes, not wanting to intrude, but anxious to help if help was needed. They had been moving for about half an hour when the questions asking themselves in her head demanded to be spoken.

"I don't understand," she blurted out. "What is it you want to do? Why can't someone go with you?"

Marheh started as if she had forgotten Gelis' presence. For a moment Gelis quailed under her gaze then she seemed to shake off the painful thoughts and smiled at her apprentice.

"I'm sorry," she said, touching her lightly. "I'll try to explain. Maybe that will help me make up my mind."

She drew a deep breath and looked ahead to where the water road beckoned.

"Many years ago, when I was about your age, my mentor and I discovered that it was possible to remove the water dimension from a mind. Until that time there was little we could do against the Yareblis except control them for a while. We didn't want to be like them and break their minds. Removing the water dimension only took away their ability to see the water road and to control. They could still live as they had done, but their power over others was diminished."

She turned to Gelis for a moment to see whether she was following.

"It is something I have done fairly often when there has been a need, but it isn't easy, especially when I will need to place a control first. Kel and I have sometimes worked together and he wants us to do that this time, but holding the water dimension becomes painful, especially if you hold more than one, because, in the Yareblis, it is distorted, twisted from the true. I want him to be in a position to receive what I take and destroy it."

She paused and looked again at Gelis who nodded slowly.

"Kel is afraid you will be left vulnerable when you're doing it, isn't he?" she said. "Couldn't I go with you?"

Marheh hesitated for a moment then spoke slowly.

"I don't see why you couldn't come part of the way at least. It depends a bit on what we can find for cover. You would have to stay hidden. Let me think about it for a bit."

Gelis nodded again then fell silent, trying to digest what Marheh had told her.

Another twenty minutes or so went by without much in the way of speech until Marheh indicated that she was ready to moor. Gelis went to take the front line and a few minutes later they were tied up beside a low hedge. *Storm Cloud* drew in behind them.

"This is about the best cover we'll get for the boats along here," Marheh said when they were together again sitting around the table on *Storm Cloud*. "That last bridge we went through carries a lane that crosses the Clanning Branch about three miles away."

"Yes, I know," Kel said shortly. "I can see that there are advantages in going from here, but not alone. You'd just be making a martyr of yourself and it isn't worth it."

"What if Gelis came with me?"

"Don't be ridiculous." Kel looked apologetically at Gelis. "She doesn't have the skills to defend herself yet, let alone anyone else."

"She could hide and watch, let you know if I'm being a martyr."

"And any help I could give would be too late by then."

He looked at Gelis and Loc, uncomfortable spectators.

"Would you two mind making yourselves scarce for a bit."

"Why? I don't have anything to hide."

"I'm not thinking of you, I'm thinking of them."

He jerked his head towards the door. Loc and Gelis scuttled off. Marheh got up as if preparing to leave herself. Kel grasped her wrist. She shook him off.

"Marheh."

She stared at him for a moment then subsided, covering her face with both hands.

"What is it you are not telling me?" he asked gently.

When she looked at him again he thought he had never seen her appear so bleak.

"They can't be left to go on," she said. "I've thought and thought. I saw what was up there where I found Toula. I felt the pain that still lingered. I experienced what was in Toula's mind. They were experimenting, trying to harvest her mind, her skills. If they had succeeded with her they would have gone on to the rest of you. Think what power that would have given them."

There were tears on her cheeks and he would have liked to hold and comfort her.

"I don't want to be a martyr. Underneath I'm terrified, but I can't let that get in the way. We have to disable as many as we can before they organise themselves to try again."

She reached across the table to him.

"Kel, they were succeeding. If we hadn't found her they would have harvested her mind."

He stood up and went around to draw her into his arms.

When he released her she was calm again. He gave her his handkerchief to wipe her eyes and blow her nose. She gave him an unsteady smile.

"Now I'd best go and apologise to Gelis and Loc, poor things. They will be wondering."

"I expect they will understand. When do you want to set out?"

63

"It will be light for quite a while yet. Perhaps an early tea and then go so I arrive in the half light and can hide in the shadows."

When she set off with Gelis a couple of hours later she seemed to have regained her usual quiet self discipline. The lane was easy walking and pleasant enough at first with trees either side.

"There is very little cover closer to the Clanning Branch though," Marheh told Gelis. "We'll find you a spot to hide before the trees disappear. I'm hoping by then we will be able to catch a glimpse of the water road and see whether the boats are there."

"What about you?" Gelis asked. "How close do you need to be? Where will you hide?"

"I'm hoping they have moored near the bridge, that would be the logical place, unless they have gone a lot further. If they have then the bridge might hide me, at first any way. It depends a bit on where the boats are."

It wasn't much of an answer but it was all she could give.

"How can I help if I'm not near you?"

Marheh did not answer for some minutes, just kept walking at the same steady pace. Gelis walked quietly beside her.

"By allowing me to take refuge in your mind if I should need to."

Gelis stopped walking in surprise then ran to catch up.

"We'll check on the boats and find you a place to hide, then I'll try to explain."

Another half hour of walking and the trees were thinning. The landscape beyond them was very flat and bare. There had been little sign of life during their walk, no vehicle, no stock grazing, just the occasion burst of bird song or the flash of wings passing. Marheh was walking a little slower now and seemed to be looking for something, a particular tree. When she stopped then walked across to touch one, Gelis understood why. It was a perfect climbing tree. Marheh studied it for a moment then swung herself onto the lowest branch and turned back to laugh at Gelis.

"I wasn't sure if I could still do it," she said. "Come on, there's room for both of us."

She was already perched on a big branch several feet higher by the time Gelis had managed the lowest level. The brief moment of enjoyment soon left her, but when Gelis joined her she smiled a welcome and shifted sideways to give her room nearest the tree trunk.

"This will be a good hiding place for you," she said. "I'll be able to picture you here."

"But…" Gelis began.

"Can you see the bridge, just a bump on the horizon and a bit to the left a glimpse of white?"

The canopy was still sparse, the new spring growth did not impede her view, but there was not much light left. Gelis thought she could make out the bump on the horizon but not the glimpse of white that Marheh obviously thought was one of the boats she sought. Then a flicker of light caught her eye. It was quickly extinguished, but enough.

She nodded.

"It's a long way still."

Marheh touched her lightly.

"Not so very far. You can see from here and watch where I go."

Gelis nodded again but did not speak. How could she help Marheh from here? Soon it would be dark and then she wouldn't even be able to see her.

"There have been times in the past," Marheh was saying when she turned attention to her. "When I needed to escape into Kel's mind, but he will be busy dealing with the water dimensions that I send him. Will you let me act from within your mind instead if I should need to?"

"Of course," Gelis said. "But how will I know?"

"Stay awake and be willing, that will be enough."

Marheh studied Gelis' face in the half light then touched her again.

"I'm glad you are here."

Before Gelis had time to form a response she had slithered down to the branch below and then below that. From the ground she paused to look up at Gelis, her face a pale oval in the dim light, then she turned and walked away.

Gelis watched her stepping out along the lane. The drab colours of her work-a-day uniform blended with the shadows and even knowing she was there, Gelis soon found it difficult to see her. She watched and watched, dashing impatiently at the tears that blurred her vision. Marheh's last words to her had seemed like a valediction, as if she thought she might not return.

She came
A lightning flash
And perfume,
Unimaginably sweet.

Then went.
Will the empty place
Remain
Forever in my mind?

Gelis

CHAPTER SIX

The small happiness of climbing the tree accompanied Marheh for a little time. She allowed herself to experience the pleasure of it, taste the memories it brought of youth and freedom. Her plan, such as it was, needed no further thought until she was close enough to put it into action and that time would come soon enough. There was no turning back.

The lane curved towards the water road and now she was close enough to see where the boats lay moored, a dozen or more, in a long double row, blocking the narrow waterway. It was almost dark and the white boats looked other worldly, like pale ghosts of themselves. Edges of light showed from some of the windows as if curtains had been imperfectly closed. It was not those she needed to worry about, but the ones with the dark spaces where hidden eyes might see her approach.

There was no one on the bank, but she held herself ready to act in case someone appeared. Better though if she could hide herself in the shadow of the bridge hole before action alerted them to her presence. If she hid within the water dimension, she reasoned, then not only would that assist her in transferring what she took from the Yareblis to Kel, but also would mean those she disabled would not be able to see her.

The odds against her were not good, but her position was not hopeless. She was practised at entering a mind without being noticed.

If she could do that and excise the ability to use the water dimension while her targets were still on their boats she hoped they would be unaware of what they lacked until, having stepped off a boat, they could no longer see to step back on again.

A good deal depended on her being able to reach the bridge unseen. There was no cover anywhere near the approach, but twilight baffled the eye and she was wearing soft, dark colours. She did not hurry, but drifted noiselessly closer, stepping carefully on the hard, compacted earth of the lane.

The closer she came to the bridge the more tempting it was to make a dash for the cover it offered, but she knew that sudden movement would catch a casual eye. A sigh of relief escaped her when she finally sank down behind the bulk of the bridge. She needed to cross it to reach the water dimension, but for the moment she could rest and listen.

It was fully dark and the moon had risen before she made her next move, confident now that she had not been observed. She crawled across the bridge, careful to keep below the balustrade, then crept around the end and down to where the towpath went beneath. The moon, though not full, was bright enough to cast deep shadow and she eased into this and sat against the wall of the heavy brick arch for a moment or two before deciding she would be less visible lying on her stomach, pressed into the angle.

The boats seemed very close now, moored only a few yards from where she lay, and it was difficult to abandon her physical self in order to begin the concentrated work of her mind. The body she inhabited would become so vulnerable once she left it. Perhaps she could wait a little, some might then be sleeping. Procrastination was not helpful. She had to begin. Would their boats provide a defence against her like the Silberay boats did for them? Her tiniest, sharpest, little probe reached out and sought entry.

It did not take her long to find a mind unguarded. For a moment she hesitated, knowing that once she began she must continue until the work was complete, or until she was forced to stop. Control, cut, carry away. The first was accomplished. She would try to contain a second before changing her focus to send what she had taken to Kel.

* * * *

For Gelis, perched up in her tree, the night was already beginning to seem very long. For a while she had been buoyed by the adventure of it and the hope that she might be of use to Marheh, but as darkness closed around her the hope and the adventure dwindled. She had thought her position, tucked in against the trunk, was both comfortable and secure, but as time went on she found herself needing to wriggle to ease the numbness in her behind. More than once her eyes closed and her head drooped before she had jolted awake in time to clutch at her branch. She thought about climbing down and walking around a bit to ease her stiffness but was not sure whether Marheh would be able to find her if she was not where she had left her. Marheh had asked her to stay awake, stay awake... stay awake...

* * * *

Once Marheh had set out Kel spent a little time appreciating the quiet evening and the peace of *Storm Cloud*, allowing this to ready him for the focused waiting to come. All sense of time passing disappeared as he held Marheh in his mind.

Then it began. She sent him two, and then another two, so quickly that he barely had time to rid himself of them in between. The next came more slowly but then came three in quick succession. The small portion of his mind that was not occupied with the work wondered at her strength. As long as these twisted fragments from Yareblis minds kept coming then he knew she was still herself, but how much was it costing her and how long could she remain hidden. Surely they must become aware of her activity amongst them.

Marheh had lost count of the minds she had entered, the changes she had made to them. She had not reached the end of the task, only the end of her strength. She had to rest for a little. If she was discovered now she would have nothing with which to resist or defend herself. She allowed her mind to ease back from its exploration and re-enter her body. Her chosen hiding place had been damp, she discovered, feeling the chill through her clothes, but it had been enough to keep her safe. Cautiously she stretched as best she could without changing her position. She was very stiff. How long had she been working? It was still night, or perhaps early morning. She thought the moon shadow had shifted.

How many more? When she began again it would be more difficult. She was tired and the ones left were those who were best defended. It would not be easy to act without them being aware of her. Perhaps it would be sensible to leave now while she still could. There would be confusion enough when those she had disabled left the boats. Almost she could feel sorry for them, suddenly homeless, here in the middle of nowhere.

Carefully she eased herself into a sitting position, then stood, rather unsteadily and leaned against the bulk of the bridge. Just putting one foot after the other would be as much as she could manage now, more than she could manage perhaps. She practised a little, lifting one foot and then the other on the spot while her weary mind tried to grasp the necessary action. Then she set off to crawl back across the bridge.

Getting to her feet again on the other side she stumbled a little. A stone fell into the water with a small splash. Just go. Her mind was still having trouble directing her legs, but she pushed herself on as best she could, suddenly feeling conspicuous in the moonlight.

A hundred difficult yards later the attack came. There was nowhere to run had she been capable of running and there was no strength left in her mind for fighting. Some instinct had her drop to the ground before she gathered her mind to flee the attacker. Not Kel, Gelis. Gelis was waiting for her. She found her and made the leap into the shelter of her mind. Not for long, she couldn't stay for long. They would be seeking her and she must not draw them to her apprentice, but she could remain hidden for a few minutes, long enough to breath and think.

Gelis felt Marheh's arrival like a bolt of lightening, a moment of pain, a burst of brightness, a shining that filled her with warmth and optimism. Marheh needed her. Marheh trusted her enough to yield her mind to her keeping. Could love keep her safe? Could she give Marheh some of her strength? Was it enough to want to give or was there something more she needed to do?

And then she was gone again, the brightness fading. Gelis opened her eyes and gazed into the darkness. Where was she? What was she confronting?

The full power of the Yareblis attack turned on Marheh as she

70

offered herself. She would not hide again. If she had learned anything, achieved any wisdom, acquired the ability to love enough, then these would be her weapons and her strength. Where once she had become the shining warrior princess, now she was nothing, less than nothing, a woman, naked and vulnerable. The attack beat at her mind, blow upon blow. Within the pain she remained steady, drawing in the sharp, wounding blows and returning them changed, transformed into love, the love she felt for the Silberay, for her family, for the village, even, though she had not known it until now, the love she felt for her enemies who could have been Silberay had they so chosen.

There seemed no end to the agony that must pass through her to be wrenched around, translated, remade and sent back as warmth, affection, care and love. She seemed to be alone, immobilised, frozen in an empty desert of pain, but gradually the love she was offering drew other loves to itself to warm and enrich her giving. Then, without any intent on her part, she was singing and the love was the song and the song was warmth and light and the agony fell away powerless against her.

* * * *

Kel, waiting and wondering on *Storm Cloud*, felt increasingly anxious when several hours passed and she had sent nothing more. Surely she would have let him know if she had finished what she had set out to do. About an hour before dawn he could wait no longer. Leaving a note for Loc he set out along the lane she had taken with Gelis. His long strides covered the ground quickly and even amongst the trees the moon gave enough light to show him the way.

Gelis too was anxious. Marheh had left her so long ago. She kept straining to see, looking along the lane where she had watched her walk so calmly into danger. Was there, perhaps, a faint lightening of the sky in the east? If dawn was approaching surely she would be justified in climbing down from her tree and going to look for her.

She had almost made up her mind to descend when she saw movement on the lane, coming towards her. Then the movement resolved itself into two figures. As they approached she heard them arguing then they passed beneath her.

"We should have gone the other way," said one.

"Go then, I'm not stopping you," said the other.

But they both plodded on.

As soon as they were out of sight and out of earshot Gelis climbed carefully down and set off along the lane. She had been right about the sky. It was definitely lighter now although the sun was not yet up. She could see the white boats lined up and, as she watched, one, then another, moved away under the bridge and out of sight along the Clanning Branch.

She had almost reached the long curve that turned the lane towards the water road when she saw another figure walking towards her. A moment of hope before she realised that the shape was not Marheh's. The person was bigger, bulkier altogether, a man, she decided.

She kept walking, telling herself she was foolish to be afraid of a stranger. Then she saw him stop and step back as if he had seen something unexpected. She thought perhaps there was a fallen log on the path or ... or. She saw him spit and raise one foot and kick and suddenly she understood what he saw.

"No-o-o!" she screamed, running towards him. "No!"

He lowered the foot that had been raised to kick again and turned towards her. She skidded to a stop in front of him too angry and upset to be afraid.

"Get away from her," she shouted.

The man sneered and was about to push her aside when he seemed to see something behind her that changed his mind.

"Bitch!"

He spat then turned and stomped away. In a moment Gelis was on her knees beside Marheh. She was pale and dirty and so still. Sobbing her name Gelis tried to lift her, turn her so she could pillow her head on her lap. She was crying so hard she didn't hear Kel's approach and started when he suddenly appeared, kneeling opposite her on Marheh's other side.

"I think she's dead," she sobbed. "And he kicked her."

Kel shook his head. He thought he would know if she had left them, but he reached for the wrist nearest him to feel for a pulse.

"Not dead," he said quietly. "But perhaps damaged, or lost in the song."

Gelis stared at him not really understanding.

"I think we should make her as comfortable as we can and then sing with her."

He was remembering another time when she had suffered and found respite in the song and lost the thread that linked soul to mind and body.

"What about...?" Gelis looked towards the white boats that remained.

"Many have been disabled, and her song will persuade any others away."

"I think it already has," she said.

He smiled at her and lifted Marheh gently onto her side, tucking his coat under her head.

"Hold her hand," he said. "Touch will help her find us."

* * * *

Marheh bathed and warmed herself in the song that surrounded her. Suffering became a memory. Harmony enfolded her, polishing her melody so that it shone out, more golden, more beautiful, more loving and beloved. She wanted to remain within the comfort of it and for a time it was possible but then she felt herself called to different music. One song held a steady anchoring pulse that offered a ground for her melody. She could allow it to become her rhythm. The other song was unpractised, simple notes that yearned for more knowledge, for her knowledge. She was called to complete this stumbling tune. Gently she placed her song beneath it, lifting it, holding back her own song and offering herself to nurture the other.

When the song ended the three singers found that the sun had risen, flooding the fields with light. Marheh was bruised and sore both mentally and physically, but she had opened her eyes and recognised her companions. Kel and Gelis were more alert, kept on edge by noise and confusion coming from the water road and the white boats. It seemed to be unrelated to their own presence however and after a few thoughtful minutes Kel realised what was happening.

"Marheh has disabled them," he explained to Gelis. "They got off the boats and now they can't find them to get back on again."

"Oh."

Gelis looked curiously towards the boats and saw figures on the bank. Would they try to return to Deerford? The men she had seen earlier must have come from the boats too.

They watched anxiously for some time, wondering whether they were at risk of retribution, but although two or three came past them along the lane only one seemed to recognise them and he just sneered and continued. Another five or six went in the other direction, away from the bridge.

"Are they all gone?" Gelis wondered, when ten minutes or so had passed with no sign of life.

"Possibly."

Kel knew how many had been disabled, but not how many there had been to begin with. Marheh seemed to be sleeping peacefully but he was aware of the toll her activities would have taken. Her mind would be unable to function normally for some time.

"We can't stay here," he said, thinking aloud. "But I don't think I'm capable of carrying Marheh back to *Day Bringer*, not now."

"I could go back for Loc," Gelis offered.

"You could, but..." He stood up. "Will you stay with Marheh? I'm just wondering whether we might make use of one of the Yareblis boats."

Gelis nodded and watched anxiously while he strode away. What would he find? Were the Yareblis all gone? She saw him walk along the line of boats, stopping sometimes to peer through a window. She looked at Marheh, resting beside her and thought about the song she had just experienced. She understood now that the distant glory that had come close to nourish her simple tune had been Marheh's song. Would she wake and be restored? The loss of her mentor when she had barely begun to know her was unthinkable.

Then Kel was on his way back.

"All empty as far as I can tell," he said. "I think we would be justified in using one of them to get Marheh back to *Day Bringer*, don't you?"

Gelis grinned and nodded.

"I'd best warn Loc though," he said then and Gelis saw him turn inwards, focusing for a few moments.

She and Marheh might be able to communicate that way one day.

"Now," he said. "I wonder whether I can still lift her."

He knelt and put his arms underneath her. Gelis saw the strain on his face as he staggered to his feet. She looked at him anxiously then bent to pick up his coat. He was already striding towards the boats. Gelis ran after him.

"Which one?"

"The nearest, but be careful, just in case."

The words jerked out of him.

She ran ahead, stopped beside the closest *Boat A*nd peered through the windows before stepping on board. It looked as if someone had just finished breakfast. There was a bowl in the small sink and a cup on the little table. The layout was very different from *Day Bringer*. Perhaps it would be easiest to lay Marheh on the deck. She grabbed a cushion and went out with it in time to put it under Marheh's head as Kel put her down.

"Is there a blanket?" he asked.

Gelis went off to look while he went to familiarise himself with the controls, a steering wheel, not a tiller, but there was a key in the ignition and when he turned it the engine burst into life. Gelis emerged from below with a blanket to put carefully over Marheh before stepping off to undo the mooring lines then the boat eased away from the bank.

It took Kel a few minutes of experimenting before he felt comfortable enough to turn the boat. He steered under the bridge where Marheh had hidden to where the water road was a little wider then swung the *Boat A*round. Gelis sat on the deck beside Marheh, watching the rise and fall of her breathing and wondering what she had done that had taken such a toll on her. She was curious about the boat they had borrowed too. It some ways it had a temporary feel to it, not the homelike solidarity of *Day Bringer*, but the fittings were good quality. It was just rather soulless, not unlike the YRTHA building, which made sense if the Yareblis did not acknowledge the soul.

It took about an hour to get back to their own boats. Kel was being extra careful with property that was not his own. Loc was waiting to help them moor, obviously pleased to see them safely back. Marheh had not moved during the short journey and Gelis was becoming more and more anxious about her.

"What have they done to her? Why is she like this?" she whispered to Kel as he stood looking down at them both.

"It will be the consequence of the battle she fought," he said.

He crouched down and spoke her name.

"She will recover better and be more comfortable on *Day Bringer*."

Gelis nodded.

"Shall I go and open her cabin doors?"

As she left she heard him say her name again, calling to her with such gentleness and love that she needed to blink back sudden tears.

By the time she had returned Marheh had opened her eyes. Kel had lifted her a little and held her against him.

"Will you ask Loc to come please. It will be easier with both of us."

Off she went again, wondering what exactly was wrong, why Marheh could not just get up and walk.

It was Loc who explained.

Once Marheh had been carefully conveyed to her cabin he suggested giving Gelis breakfast on *Storm Cloud*. She discovered she was ravenous and went with him gladly, recognising that Kel needed to be with Marheh.

"I don't altogether understand it either," he said between

mouthfuls of scrambled egg. "But I've seen something similar with Kel, just once, after a Yareblis challenge. He told me afterwards that the mind can't always recover quickly. Sometimes everyday things need to be relearned. Marheh is much better at it than anyone else but it costs her more too I think."

By lunch time Marheh was recovered enough to sit in the armchair on *Day Bringer* and sip at a mug of sperit. She could smile at Gelis and thank her for allowing her to take refuge in her mind. After they had eaten Kel and Loc went off on the white boat, planning to return it to the Clanning Branch and come back on foot. Gelis spent the afternoon cooking an evening meal they could share and watching over Marheh as she rested in the armchair. Once, when she looked up from peeling carrots, she saw Marheh was watching her.

"I'm making supper," she explained, feeling oddly awkward.

Marheh smiled and nodded.

"I'll be glad of it."

"Can I get you anything now?"

"Not now."

She looked towards the footstool beside her chair.

"Can you come and sit for a few minutes?"

Gelis nodded and put down her peeler. When she was seated Marheh continued.

"I'm very grateful for all you have done."

She paused for a moment and Gelis saw a spark of amusement that hinted at the return of the Marheh she knew.

"And for all you are doing and will do, because you're a good girl and your mentor is getting old and tired."

Gelis grinned and shook her head.

"But you've really been plunged in at the deep end and there must be questions you want answers for, things you want to know."

"Loc and Kel have been really kind," Gelis said slowly. "They've explained some things. I'm still trying to make sense of what they told me and of all that has happened. I know there will be more questions but I'm not quite sure what they are yet."

"Fair enough," Marheh said, smiling at her. "Just ask when you're ready. Now I have a question for you."

She paused for a moment and Gelis looked up at her.

"Do I have a dirty face?"

It was so unexpected that Gelis began to laugh.

"That's better," Marheh said. "You were looking very solemn before. Come on, tell me the worst."

"It was dirty when we found you," she said. "I think Kel must have tried to wash it. Now you just look a bit patchy."

She laughed again as Marheh made a face.

"Shall I bring you a washer?"

"No thank you, you can help me to the bathroom. It's time I made an effort to find myself again."

White Boats

CHAPTER SEVEN

The evening meal became a celebration because Marheh was herself again. Only Kel recognised something of what it was costing her to smile and laugh and make a joke or two, mocking herself when her mind needed reminding how to use a spoon. Even he knew nothing of the painful bruise on her hip. Loc and Gelis waited on their mentors gladly, pleased to see them enjoy the meal Gelis had prepared and happy to be helping them to relax and recover from the effort of the previous night.

While the two apprentices were tackling the washing up, Marheh and Kel remained at the table, sitting opposite each other, hand linked, communicating quietly without need of words. Kel shared his deep affection, his love and admiration for her courage and skill. Marheh gave him her love and gratitude for his care and strength. For both of them was the weight of knowledge that the struggle was not ended.

"Come and join us," Kel invited, when the dishes were done and mugs of sperit distributed.

"We need your thoughts," Marheh added.

She turned to Gelis.

"Kel told me you saw some Yareblis boats leaving?"

Gelis nodded.

"Two of them at least. They went under the bridge and away along the water road."

"Towards Clanning?" Marheh asked.

"In the direction they were pointing. They didn't turn as far as I could see."

"We have to decide whether or not to pursue then," Kel said. "I think Marheh has done enough for the moment and you two have experiences you need time to make sense of, but the Clanning Branch ends at Clanning, and if they stay with the boats then by moving to the junction we could restrict their movement."

"I'd really like to follow them into the Clanning Branch itself," Marheh said. "I don't think they'll stay with the boats for long, but the Clanning Branch is... difficult at best. Their numbers have been significantly reduced, perhaps we have done enough for the moment."

Gelis and Loc looked at each other. Were they really being asked for their opinion?

"What do you think Gelis," Loc asked. "All this must have been pretty challenging for you."

Gelis looked around the table at these new friends.

"I don't think I know enough to have an opinion really, but would it be ... The junction can't be far, maybe we could go there in case and then make up our minds."

"Sounds sensible to me," Kel said, smiling at Gelis.

"And me," Marheh said. "Let's go then."

"Now!"

Gelis and Loc spoke together. Kel's cautionary tone as he spoke Marheh's name was almost lost in the sound.

"Why not?" Her eyes held a hint of challenge as she looked around the table. "It isn't far and it's a nice night."

"And you are not fully fit and it is already 10 o'clock."

"What an old grump you are. It will be fun." She turned to the two apprentices. "Won't it?"

They looked at each other and grinned. It would of course, especially with Marheh in this mood, but they were not quite ready to acknowledge it.

Kel laughed.

"What chance has the voice of commonsense!"

A few minutes later all signs of the meal they had shared were cleared away. Kel and Loc had departed to *Storm Cloud* and Marheh was supervising while Gelis did the engine checks. They heard the sound of *Storm Cloud*'s engine starting up. Gelis slid the dip stick back into place and followed Marheh out to the back deck. Loc was just a dark shape on the bank. He was already coiling the front line, holding himself ready to push off when Kel gave the nod.

"He must have cheated," Marheh said loudly, deliberately provoking.

Gelis giggled and jumped off to run to *Day Bringer*'s prow. *Storm Cloud* slid past them, Loc standing in the well deck waving, Kel at the tiller.

"Slow coach," he said as he came level with Marheh.

She saw the flash of teeth as he grinned at her and laughed as she started the engine and nodded to Gelis to push off.

It was a lovely night, still and quiet with only the gentle throbbing of the engines disturbing the peace. Gelis, standing beside Marheh on the back deck, thought she had never seen so many stars. The water road reflected them back, sparkling in the darkness. Spreading ripples from *Storm Cloud*'s wake shimmered.

She looked at Marheh, her hand light on the tiller, her eyes focused ahead and sighed a little at the beauty of it all. Marheh turned to her then, for a moment, and smiled in sympathy.

An hour later they arrived at the junction. For Marheh the journey had been too short. The thinking time at the tiller had helped her healing but not allowed her to reach any decision about the way forward. She was tempted to accept the partial victory they had achieved and resume her ordinary practice, travelling, working and singing light. It would be some time before she was fully recovered from her recent exertions. Beneath her pretence at normality she was tired and drained. Her mind seemed to her to be fumbling and clumsy when she needed sharpness and clarity. Even her song seemed dimmed, needing the songs of others to help it shine.

"But we can't give up now."

Gelis looked at her and she realised she had spoken her thought.

"Sometimes, in the past, we have had to settle for less than we would like," she went on, deliberately speaking to Gelis this time. "Now we might have a chance to do better than that."

"You want to go after them don't you?"

"Most of me does." She smiled. "There's a lazy coward hanging around trying to convince me that we have done enough."

"Well it isn't you and I don't think it's me," Gelis said. "So that makes two against one."

Marheh laughed.

"So it does. It must be bedtime now, but in the morning we'll gang up and toss her overboard."

Gelis smiled then looked earnestly at Marheh.

"I'll help as much as I can, what ever you decide."

"I know you will. Thank you."

She saw the concern and affection on Gelis' face and impulsively opened her arms. The hug was a gift and a promise.

"Good night, sleep well."

* * * *

Morning came before Marheh was ready for it but she pushed herself out of bed and went to wash as usual. Then she made herself sperit and took it out to the well deck where she could sit and study the entrance to the Clanning Branch. It held so many memories, not many of them good. Her dear Nemle, her mentor, had disliked and avoided it until they had been give a job to do that took them there.

They had succeeded in their task, but not without cost. A shiver of apprehension surprised her as she contemplated past and possible future.

Nemle, she had been gone for so long now but there were still times when missing her was like a pain. There had been times when Nemle had tried to shield her. Their task in Clanning had been one of them. How she had resented it and now she was doing the same to Gelis.

"But," she tried to excuse herself. Then honesty forced her to recognise that the situation was not really so different.

She still found it difficult to accept that she was a mentor now. Gelis had been the only new apprentice and she had been chosen to mentor her, not Tippa her contemporary amongst the Silberay. She was lucky really, an apprentice was the future. *Day Bringer* would pass from her to Gelis in due course and continue to live even when she did not.

"I'll do my very best," she said aloud, knowing she was promising Nemle as well as Gelis.

She felt *Day Bringer* move beneath her and realised Gelis was up and about. Breakfast then. She stood up and went inside. After breakfast they would consult with Kel and Loc and hopefully make some decisions. If only she didn't feel so muddled, so unsure of the way ahead, and of herself, she realised suddenly.

She grimaced. That was new. Where was Marheh the Great when she needed her?

Gelis was in the galley stirring the porridge when she moved through from her cabin. She looked up and grinned at Marheh.

"Five minutes," she said.

"What a treasure you are."

Marheh's words were teasing, but there was a new depth of affection beneath them. She slid into her seat at the table. It was the same balancing act that Nemle had struggled with, the desire to protect and cherish had to be tempered by the need to give room for learning and growth.

Not quite an hour later they were all together, sitting in *Day*

Bringer's well deck enjoying the morning sunshine while they debated their next moves.

"If we hang around here too long they'll either regroup or leave the area altogether," Marheh said firmly, perhaps more firmly than necessary, needing to persuade herself.

"But if we act too quickly, without thinking it through, we might head off in the wrong direction and lose them anyway," Kel argued.

Gelis looked from one to the other. She didn't think she knew enough to have an opinion about the action they should take but she was beginning to recognise the way Marheh and Kel complemented each other.

"There are not many choices. We know they went towards Clanning. They would have had to be very quick to have come back to the Great Northern without us seeing."

Marheh sounded very confident.

"I was wondering whether we should perhaps travel via the WEG," Kel said. "It goes reasonably close to Clanning and we would not be as visible approaching from there."

"But they might not have gone all the way to Clanning," Marheh protested. "What if they stopped at Ponder, or anywhere else along the way?"

"How likely is that? Clanning is the only place of any size and you, more than most, know how they used Clanning before."

Marheh seemed to be hesitating and he tried to push home his argument.

"A couple of quiet days on the WEG would be good for us. We need to regain our strength too."

She studied him suspiciously.

"I have a nasty feeling you are pandering to me," she said at last. "It isn't our strength you're talking about, it's my strength." She grimaced. "You're probably right, much as I hate to admit it. I still vote for the Clanning Branch though. It would take us a week or more to get there via the WEG and that's too long."

"Can we compromise?" Kel asked. "Stay here quietly this

morning, and make our way carefully into the Clanning Branch this afternoon. Perhaps get as far as the place they moored so we can investigate the boats they left behind?"

Marheh nodded.

"Except we might as well get going and have longer to investigate the boats. You never know, we might even find something useful."

Kel shook his head.

"Obviously you are not going to rest if we stay here so we might as well get going," he said. "But we are not going further than the Yareblis boats today even if I have to bribe Gelis to hide *Day Bringer*'s keys."

Marheh raised her eyebrows and grinned at Gelis.

"We're a team. She wouldn't accept a bribe."

"Of course she wouldn't."

Kel laughed and stood up.

"Come on Loc, it looks as if we will need to get ahead of them and moor in the bridge hole if we want to keep control."

Ten minutes later they were on their way. Marheh had restrained her competitive streak and not hurried to be first so *Day Bringer* was following *Storm Cloud* about a boat length behind. Since the fleet of white boats had passed through the entrance she decided that all the wire must have gone although she had warned Kel what they had found earlier, as well as about the water at the service area. He was travelling very cautiously and she followed suit, listening hard for any hint of a problem.

Beyond the service area the way ahead looked weedy and overgrown but now she was looking with new insight and recognised the illusion.

"It wasn't like this when we came the other way," Gelis said.

"You were on one of their boats then," Marheh said. "See if you can see through it, it's an illusion."

In front, *Storm Cloud* was ploughing steadily onwards looking to Gelis almost as if she was making her way through a grassy field. She tried to remind herself what she had seen from the white boat that had carried Marheh back to *Day Bringer*. For a few moments she struggled then suddenly her vision cleared. The little gasp indicated her success. Marheh turned to her with a smile.

"Not overgrown at all," she commented. "It makes me think they have been using the Clanning Branch for a while. That should teach us that it isn't safe to neglect any part of the water road."

It was not much more than half an hour before they reached the row of white boats. The channel was very narrow beside them in the places where two were moored side by side.

"Do you think all the boats from Deerford came here?" Gelis asked as they wriggled their way through.

"I was assuming so," Marheh said. "But I didn't actually count the boats I saw there."

"I didn't either. I didn't want to look for long in case they suspected that I could see them."

They counted them now, two singles they had already passed, then a pair, breasted up, another single, another pair and two more singles.

"With the two you saw leaving that makes eleven," Marheh said. "I had a feeling there were more than that. What do you think?"

Gelis shook her head.

"There seemed like a lot, so perhaps, I can't be sure."

Marheh gave a little grunt of acknowledgement, concentrating on squeezing past the second pair.

"How many did you disable?" Gelis asked once they were clear of the boats and following *Storm Cloud* through the bridge.

"About a dozen I think. I lost count in the end. Kel would probably know."

Ahead of them Kel was mooring up, leaving enough space for *Day Bringer* to moor behind him.

Once the boats were secure the four Silberay gathered on the bank.

"Where did you hide?" Loc asked Marheh, looking around at the flat, inhospitable landscape around them.

"Under the bridge." She laughed. "There is probably an imprint still left in the mud. Come on. Let's go and take a look on the boats."

"In twos I think, don't you?" Kel said tactfully as she turned to go.

"What are we looking for?" Loc asked as they moved towards the row of Yareblis boats.

"Anything that might point to where they were going, anything that gives us a clue about numbers, anything out of place…" She broke off and grinned. "Anything at all really. I'm just a sticky beak."

Loc and Gelis laughed.

"Agreed," Kel said, smiling. "We do need to be cautious though."

Marheh put her tongue out at him then screwed up her face.

"He's right, as usual!"

She moved towards the first boat in the line, Gelis close behind her. Curtains were drawn over the window and the port hole in the prow. As she stepped on board Kel and Loc went past to board the next in line.

They took quite some time over their explorations, making sure they had investigated every possible nook and cranny, every potential hiding place. Once they had noted the differences between these boats and their own they seemed fairly ordinary on the whole. They were not nearly as spacious as the Silberay boats, without proper cabins. Only the unmade beds on one or two of them indicated the sleeping arrangements. They didn't have fires either.

"I thought they would want a bit more comfort," Gelis commented as they began the search of their third boat.

"These are fair weather boats," Marheh said, her voice muffled by the cupboard she had her head in. A moment later she sat back on her heels and dusted off her hands on the seat of her trousers. "I think you must have been right about them living in the clubhouse. Nothing much in the way of stores, no spare clothes to speak of, it certainly doesn't seem as if they were living on any boat we've seen yet."

It was Gelis who reached under the cushion of a long seat and found a wallet. She held it out to Marheh.

"If we don't look inside," Marheh said with a grin. "Then we can't find the owner."

Gelis laughed.

They didn't actually count the money, but it was well filled. More important was the driver's license it held with an address in Clanning. They took it with them when they moved to the next boat. It was on the outside of the last pair and, as soon as they stepped on board, they realised that it was fitted out with much more care and expense than the others they had been on.

Marheh stood still on the deck for a few minutes. Gelis thought she seemed to be listening for something and waited quietly beside her.

"I can't catch it," she said at length. "But we'll need to look extra carefully here."

When they stepped down into the saloon they made their first find. Spread out on the small table was a map of Deerford. It was annotated with a range of symbols that they would need time to translate but even at first glance Marheh could see how the pottery had been highlighted. She folded it carefully and put it in her pocket then stood looking about the neatly fitted out space.

On one of the bulkheads, just at eye level, was a small shelf.

"I don't think they had time to be subtle," she said to Gelis, reaching up.

She took down several small fat books with carbon paper showing at the edges and three or four neatly folded charts and maps.

"I think we had better take all of these. We'll need to study them together. I'm not very smart when it comes to account books."

"Not?" Gelis teased.

"Not." Marheh laughed. "I'm very good with maps though," she said, exaggerating her tone to mock herself a little.

They piled the things on the table and continued to search, but although they were careful to turn out every drawer and put their heads into every cupboard they found nothing else useful. Marheh debated with herself about the ethics of taking the half bottle of milk that stood on the counter beside the sink and decided that it would only go to waste if she didn't, so that went with them too when they returned to *Day Bringer* with their discoveries.

Marheh opened the table top so all four could be accommodated and spread out one of the charts while Gelis made sperit. Kel and Loc had joined them by the time the kettle had boiled.

"Quite a haul," Kel commented.

"We haven't looked yet, not really. Everything was on one boat so we just brought it here to study. Did you find anything?"

"Nothing like this."

"We really need someone like Chanra or Yarla to look at the books, but we should be able to learn something from the charts."

She tapped the one she had opened out.

"How dare they have a map of the water road! Where would they get it from? None of us would have given it to them. I wonder what these symbols mean."

Kel bent over to examine the small shapes that dotted the lines representing the water road.

"Perhaps showing where they've placed an illusion," he suggested. "Quite a lot are beside bridges."

"Maybe."

She spread a second map over the first and together they bent over it.

"Streets and buildings," Loc said. "A town, but no name that I can see."

"What's that?" Gelis put her finger on a row of letters.

"That," Kel said rather scornfully, "Is Clanning written in mirror writing. Why would they bother?"

"It is Clanning," Marheh said. "There's the pond and the water road and there's the town hall, but that writing is all reversed too."

"And there are more symbols, different ones," Gelis said.

"What was the address on the license, do you remember?" Marheh asked.

"Baggers Lane, number seven, I think. Why?"

"I just wondered whether it was marked in any way."

Together they poured over the map. Kel was the one to find Baggers Lane. He obviously had no difficulty reading the back to front letters. It did not appear to be a very long street and there was a neat little triangle marked about a third of the way along it.

"Maybe all the triangles show where Yareblis are living," Gelis said.

"It certainly seems a good possibility," Kel said.

"How many are there?" Marheh asked.

"I've found another three."

Altogether they found eight triangles. Marheh went and found her coloured pencils so they could mark them. They seemed to be clustered on the north side of the town. The triangles were not the only symbols. As well there were circles, both outlined and filled in and squares, outlined and with a cross inside them.

They made several suggestions for the meaning of these, but they all knew they were only guessing.

"We need to go and see," Marheh said.

"Not today," Kel said.

"It wouldn't hurt to move on a bit," Marheh protested.

"You need to be fully fit."

Kel looked at her for a few moments then took a thin roll of paper from the front of his tunic and spread it over the map.

It looked like some kind of bulletin, all done in mirror writing, badly reproduced but not illegible. He turned it over and there, quite large, on the other side, was a picture of a much younger Marheh. She made a little sound, not quite a gasp, not quite a whimper. Beneath the picture, in large letters, was written DANGER APPROACH WITH EXTREME CAUTION. Kel read out the caption quietly, without emphasis. Marheh lifted her chin and tried to hide behind Marheh the Great, but let him hold her for a minute or two. Gelis and Loc looked at each other.

"Wow!" Loc said, breaking the silence. "And we actually know you."

Marheh turned her face from Kel's chest and managed to grin at him. Kel tightened his hold for a moment before letting her go.

"It was a shock to me too," he said.

"As if I was some kind of wild animal," Marheh said. "Or a criminal." She bent over the paper then turned to Kel. "You read it. I can't concentrate."

Kel sat down and pulled the paper closer.

"It seems to be a news sheet. There is a date, last February, and an indication that it comes out quarterly. This column is headed 'Signs of Success'."

He pointed to the single column on the right of Marheh's picture and slowly read out the words. The last paragraph concluded *'We now have a good supply of sillies to work with and there is every indication that harvesting the power of their minds will be achievable.'*

"And that was back in February," Marheh said quietly, breaking the silence that lingered after he had finished speaking.

"And thanks to you and Gelis, they did not succeed," Loc said.

"But they are going to keep trying unless we can stop them," Marheh said.

Another silence greeted her words.

"Does it say any more about me?" she asked.

"Just that you are very skilled and strong and they should be wary of tackling you," Kel said, not quite meeting her eyes.

"Read it out properly. I need to know."

"Do you?"

"Yes." Marheh sounded quite fierce.

Loc and Gelis looked at each other. What was Kel keeping from her?

Slowly Kel began to read.

"This silly is known to have disabled more than twenty of our people. Stopping it is our highest priority. It has the ability to defeat any number of illusions and has been instrumental in destroying projects in which we have invested time, money and personnel. It should not be approached single handed. Its capture or elimination will be rewarded."

"They could at least have said 'she'." Marheh tried for lightness. "It doesn't change anything, not really, just confirms what I thought I knew."

She picked up the maps and began to fold them.

"I'm starving. Let's have lunch then go on as far as the locks."

She turned away, very brisk and businesslike, and tucked the folded maps onto the shelf next to *Day Bringer*'s charts. Loc and Gelis looked at Kel who shook his head very slightly.

"Lunch is a good idea," he said. "Do you want to share our soup?"

Marheh stood with her back to them. Kel knew her well enough to understand that she was struggling for control.

"That sounds like a good offer," she said, without turning around.

"I'll go and get it started," Loc said, gesturing for Gelis to go with him.

When they were alone Kel went to her and put his arms around her. He felt her quiver and tightened his hold.

"Sorry," she said, after a few minutes. "You shouldn't indulge me."

"I'm not. Believe it or not I enjoy hugging you."

She laughed then.

"I don't know why it was such a shock. I've known I've been a target for years now."

"Seeing it written like that is a different kind of knowing."

She nodded.

"It's how they work, isn't it, making me into a non-person." She eased back from him. "I won't let them. Come on. Let's have lunch."

After they had eaten they did move on for an hour, but only after they had examined the Yareblis map, found the Clanning Branch and chosen a spot to moor that had no symbols of any kind. Kel vetoed going as far as the locks because using them would make them vulnerable and Marheh, although reluctant to admit it, knew she needed more time for her mind to recover.

Their chosen mooring turned out to be in the middle of nowhere. The land on their right, that had once been extensively mined, still lay neglected, covered in weeds with piles of clay and slag breaking the otherwise flat terrain. To their left was a little more evidence of cultivation, but few trees and no sign of habitation except a drift of smoke on the horizon.

There was plenty of time for them to sing together before the evening meal. Kel insisted that the song be focused on healing for Marheh and she reluctantly accepted that she should not try to extend her music into the darkness they both knew would be evident beyond their own light.

"Use it to teach Gelis, if you like," he said. "But not to challenge the dark."

It had been worthwhile, she thought, as sleep took her once the song had ended.

The others slept for a little too, but were careful not to wake Marheh, so that it was not until the smell of cooking drifted into her dreams that she surfaced. For a little while she lay drowsing still, the memory of the song and the care the other singers had given her, still strong within her. Then she pushed back the blanket someone, Gelis, she supposed, had put over her, stretched and got up, feeling restored and refreshed.

They were eating on *Day Bringer*. Marheh emerged to find the others all on board. Gelis was setting the table, Loc was stirring something on the stove and Kel was in the armchair studying one of the charts they had found. He began to get up when he saw her but she waved him back and took the footstool beside him. For a moment or two he studied her face.

"Much better thank you," she said, answering his unspoken

question. "What are you thinking?"

"If you are truly recovered," he said slowly. "Then we could perhaps consider investigating one of the places where the chart shows a symbol."

She nodded.

"Not until morning," he went on before she could speak. "But look…" He pointed out a place on the chart not far ahead. "We could be there in an hour."

She nodded again.

"It's a very good idea," she said. "If we could work out what the symbols mean we would be much better prepared."

They smiled at each other. She put a hand on his knee. He covered it with one of his.

"Dinner's ready."

Loc's call from the galley brought them back and they got up and went to the table.

Is it real?
You must learn to see.
That's what my mentor
Said to me.

Is it true?
You must learn to hear.
Know truth from lies.
Is danger near?

Illusion or trap
Both catch the unaware.
Listen well, look,
Learn to see what is there.

Gelis

CHAPTER EIGHT

Gelis was finding sleep elusive. She had enjoyed working with Loc to prepare their evening meal and enjoyed the compliments Marheh and Kel had given them, but the conversation afterwards and the singing before had both been unsettling.

The singing, or at least her part in it, had been disappointing. She had wanted so much to be of use to Marheh, to help her, and instead she had been helped. Now as she thought back, she knew it had been Marheh's song that had encouraged and strengthened hers. She wished there had been time to talk about it but of course it had been more important to let Marheh sleep.

At least she had been able to put the blanket over her. She had looked so vulnerable sleeping. Gelis thought perhaps she would not have wanted to be seen that way so she had been careful not to linger. Her thoughts went round and round. Perhaps she should try to sing instead of puzzling about Marheh.

It had been interesting hearing them talk about where the photograph of Marheh might have come from, and the map. An old Silberay called Blin had been obsessed with Marheh and taken many photographs without her being aware. Marheh had remembered that he had been befriended by someone called Mr Casey, who had turned out to be Yareblis. She and Kel had decided that both map and photograph had come from that time. Blin was long dead now and Marheh had disabled Mr Casey, but the photograph was not recent.

It had been a nasty shock for Marheh to see it in the Yareblis bulletin. Why would someone who had chosen to be Silberay give Marheh's picture to the Yareblis? Marheh and Kel had not really gone into that. Obviously just choosing to be Silberay was not enough on its own. You had to work at living the life. That meant singing. That was what she should be doing now. She tried to picture the evening star that she had discovered was her portal.

Next thing she knew it was morning. She could feel *Day Bringer* shifting at her mooring and realised Marheh was already up. Marheh was always up first. It was a good sign. She pushed back the covers and scrambled into her clothes. They were going to investigate the symbol and she wanted to be ready.

Marheh had the breakfast well under way, but Gelis was in time to set the table. Marheh gave her a smile and a nod of thanks but did not speak until they were sitting opposite each other with their porridge and sperit.

"Can you make do with just a wash for the next few days?" she asked first. "I think we need to be careful with our water until we know we can get more safely."

"Of course."

"I'm sorry I've been a bit limp the last few days," she went on. "Thank you for the singing. It really helped."

"But I couldn't do it," Gelis blurted out. "You had to help me."

"You were doing it, and you know, because you were there singing, and your song needed mine to complete it, it helped me to forget myself." She gave Gelis a little grin. "And that was all to the good."

They set off soon after breakfast, following *Storm Cloud*. There was no need to confer until they reached the place that had been marked where they planned to stop and investigate. Marheh even offered Gelis the tiller.

"I've been hogging the steering the last few days," she said. "Your turn now."

She didn't go in though and Gelis thought she might be doing what she called listening with her heart, but perhaps she was just enjoying the pleasant morning.

When Kel signalled that he was going to moor Gelis expected Marheh to take the tiller again but instead she made her way along the gunnel and took up the front line.

"You know what to do," Gelis heard her say. "You'll be fine."

Day Bringer bumped the bank a bit harder than usual, but Marheh was off with the front line and holding on while Gelis manoeuvred the stern in to where she could step off too.

"Not bad. I'll have to make sure you get some more practice."

Kel and Loc strolled back to them as they finished mooring.

"So what are we thinking?" Marheh asked, having put her mallet back in its place in the well deck. "An illusion?"

"It's certainly a possibility," Kel answered.

They all stood looking towards the bridge that crossed the water road a boat length ahead of *Storm Cloud*.

"We'll need to go closer then." Marheh looked at Gelis. "You might be the first to feel it because you're not as practised at seeing through them. We'll keep you safe."

Gelis nodded. She wasn't afraid, not really, not with Marheh beside her.

Kel led the way along the tow path past *Storm Cloud* towards the bridge. He stopped again a couple of yards before the arch. Both he and Marheh seemed to be listening intently.

"I would have thought we might have experienced it by now," Marheh murmured.

She looked at Gelis, who shook her head. There was no monstrous bird for her to battle, no quicksand waiting to swallow her. They took a couple more steps forward, Kel still leading. He paused with one hand on the arch and was just about to go

97

underneath when Marheh shouted his name. As he turned back something dark and heavy fell from under the bridge and thudded onto the path.

They stood stunned for a moment. It was no illusion. Then Marheh was in front of Kel, looking up into his face, one hand on each of his arms.

"How did you know?" he asked.

She shook her head. She had been listening with her heart, but so had he.

"You're alright?" she asked.

"Yes."

They moved back a couple of paces to where Gelis and Loc stood.

"A booby trap," Kel said. "Not an illusion."

"Do you think we would have triggered it if we'd been going through on *Storm Cloud*?" Loc asked.

Kel shrugged.

"Who knows? It wouldn't have done any harm, falling on the path."

"Perhaps it isn't the only one," Marheh said.

"Wouldn't their own boats have triggered it if it worked from the water?" Gelis asked.

There were no easy answers to any of their questions.

They spent several minutes examining the bridge, the sides and the top, trying to find the mechanism that had activated the trap but without success. Kel approached the arch again.

"I put my hand here," he said, resting it again on the brick by his left shoulder. "Then I ducked my head and went to go under."

Very carefully he reached up with his right hand. He was tall enough, here at the lowest part of the arch, to touch the aging brickwork above him.

"This is where it came from," he said, feeling around the hole.

"But I can't tell what triggered it."

He looked at Marheh.

"What do you think? Is there another that the boats might set off?"

She listened in silence for a minute or two then shook her head.

"I don't think so, but I can't be sure."

"Then we'd best continue," Kel said. "At least we know now what that symbol means."

Not an illusion, a trap, Gelis thought, as she followed Marheh back to *Day Bringer*, so when they came to the next one they could stop and take extra care, but it might not be the same and they had no choice, they had to go on.

Storm Cloud went slowly up to the bridge. Kel was steering, keeping dead centre, the engine barely ticking over, so that she made almost no wake. *Day Bringer* waited, ready to follow. Marheh and Gelis watching anxiously from the back deck, saw Kel send Loc below, to have the protection of *Storm Cloud*'s strong iron roof. They saw the shadow of the bridge pass over *Storm Cloud*'s prow then stripe the roof and finally, after the prow had returned to the light, the back deck, and Kel at the tiller went dark.

Kel must have been steering with his back like she had seen Marheh do, Gelis thought, seeing his silhouette with both arms raised to touch the arch above him. Nothing happened. Then it was *Day Bringer*'s turn.

"Do you want me to go inside?"

"Do you want to?"

Marheh was watching *Day Bringer* carefully. Steering was always more difficult at slow speeds.

"No."

Marheh nodded. She was concentrating fiercely in a way that told Gelis she was focusing on more than just the steering.

"Try to listen," she said. "There might be more to discover."

Gelis did her best, but was not really sure whether she was doing it properly. However, when they were through and out in the sun again, Marheh made a little grimace and shook her head.

"I'm probably being over anxious now," she said. "I don't think there was anything else to hear."

Ahead Kel was gesturing to the bank. Now they were through the bridge it was time to moor and study the Yareblis map again. Marheh muttered something under her breath. He was right to be cautious, but all this stopping and starting made for very slow progress.

"Hop down and get the chart we found," she said to Gelis, who was about to head for the front line. "Please," she added apologetically.

Gelis gave her a grin and disappeared. Marheh guided *Day Bringer* to the bank and stepped off with the centre line. They would not be staying and there was no traffic. There was no need to moor properly so why was Loc banging away with his mallet?

Gelis had returned with the chart by the time Kel had walked back to *Day Bringer*. Marheh took it and spread it out on the roof. Gelis grabbed the centre line when she let it go, but she could see there was no real need.

"We're here, right?" Marheh said one finger on the place. "That bridge was number five. That symbol was a circle with a triangle inside it. The next symbol is the opposite and it's between bridges seven and eight. Presumably that signifies something different. Let's just get going and find out."

Kel looked at her and raised his eyebrows just a little.

"Well, there's no point in hanging around, is there?"

She sounded a bit apologetic Gelis thought.

"No point at all," Kel agreed. "Unless we want to consider alternatives."

"I thought we had."

Kel nodded.

"But we could have done a bit more thinking before we left the Yareblis boats behind," he said. "I know it would cost us a bit of time, now, but there could be a real advantage in making use of the white boats to approach Clanning."

"Leave *Day Bringer* and *Storm Cloud*?"

Maybe not both of them. I just think we were a bit hasty. It would be easy enough for Loc and me to go back and get a couple of the boats, maybe the one where you found the charts and the one where we found the bulletin." He paused, watching her consider. "And I rather wish we had thought to disable the others, or at least remove the keys. If we went back we could do that."

Marheh took the chart off *Day Bringer*'s roof and began to fold it carefully. Loc and Gelis waited, looking at her a bit anxiously, but Kel understood that she was folding away her impatience along with the map. When it was done she turned to smile at them.

"I'm sorry. You'd think by now I would have a bit of self control." She looked to Gelis. "Why don't you go with them? It's a nice morning for a walk. I'll stay with the boats and use the time to give myself a talking to."

Kel smiled and touched her briefly.

"Don't be silly. There's no need for that. Better you sing, and think about how we might use the Yareblis boats."

She moved closer to him so that he put an arm around her for a quick hug.

"I shouldn't think it would take us more than an hour and a half."

She nodded.

"You'll be back in time for lunch. Bread and cheese do you?"

The three walkers set off five minutes later.

Marheh stood on *Day Bringer*'s back deck to watch them go. She wouldn't have minded a walk herself but at least this way she had time alone. When they were out of sight she made her way back to her cabin and opened the doors to the well deck. She was cross with herself for displaying her impatience. She could sit in the well deck and sing for a while and the attempt would force her to let go of her mood but more than that it would help her to come to terms with the picture that had come into her mind as she thought about Kel's proposal to get two of the white boats. She could see herself on *Day*

Bringer, being escorted by a white *Boat* Behind and before, a captive of the Yareblis. It would be the best possible use of the Yareblis boats, but the idea of pretending to be their prisoner was forcing her to confront again the emotions the words in the Yareblis bulletin had aroused.

She settled herself on the bench against the bulkhead and spent a few minutes concentrating on her breathing and allowing the sunshine to flow into her. While planning how to use the song was never certain she hoped this time to stretch herself, singing light outwards into the dark places, offering her weaknesses as well as her strengths, wanting her fears and failings stripped away for a time at least.

The song went well. When it ended she rested in the peace and purpose she had found there. There had been other singers whose music strengthened her song, allowing it to voyage into the emptiness and spread some warmth and light. They were so forgiving, the other singers. She got up to go inside and begin some lunch preparation. Her song was taken and transformed, lifted and enriched by the harmonies and counter melodies of the Silberay who sang with her.

She put a handful of rice into a saucepan of stock and began to peel and chop vegetables. The others would be hungry after their walk and soup would help the bread and cheese.

Had Gelis realised that she had sent her away? She wouldn't want to have hurt her. She and Loc seemed to get on well, so perhaps she had been glad to go with them. She had not given her any practice with the discipline of the mind for too long. Her own preoccupations and the weariness and disorientation that plagued her after engaging with the Yareblis should not have been allowed to excuse her from her responsibility to her apprentice.

The soup was bubbling nicely and she was just unfolding the table top ready for guests when the two white boats slid past. Even though she was expecting them to be in friendly hands she experienced a moment of apprehension and was glad when Gelis came running back to help with the lunch.

"You've made soup! Yum. I'm hungry."

"Did you enjoy the walk?"

Gelis nodded.

"And the ride back. Kel let me steer part of the way. You don't have to be out in the weather to drive those boats. They had a cockpit and a steering wheel. Our way is nicer though, more real somehow."

She was busy setting the table as she spoke. Marheh got out bowls and plates and handed over the loaf and the cheese. She was just giving the soup a final stir when Kel and Loc arrived each carrying a folding stool. Kel also held a bowl with fruit and Loc had *Storm Cloud*'s biscuit tin. Marheh welcomed them, meeting Kel's questioning gaze with a smile and a nod.

After they had eaten was time enough to discuss the way forward. They would still need to go carefully and investigate the meaning of the symbols but now they had the use of the Yareblis boats to consider. Marheh was prepared.

"A boat in front of *Day Bringer* and one behind with me in the middle pretending to be a prisoner," she said firmly.

Kel looked at her.

"You know that's the best way to get close. You probably thought of it yourself."

Kel nodded.

"Are you sure?"

She smiled at him.

"How much safer could I be with you and Loc and Gelis all looking out for me?"

How soon should the charade begin was the next question. If they needed to stop and investigate the symbols it would be a couple of days before they approached Clanning. They still had a flight of locks to ascend and that would take an hour or so more with three boats to manage, or four if they were still using *Storm Cloud*.

"If you're happy to leave *Storm Cloud*, I think we should start at once," Marheh said at last.

Happy was the wrong word. Kel would feel about leaving *Storm Cloud* the way she would feel about leaving *Day Bringer*. She looked at

103

him sympathetically.

"I should have said reconciled to leaving her."

"I expected it to have to happen," Kel said. "You'd better give time for Loc and me to get a few necessities and make sure we leave her comfortable."

"What do you want me to do?" Gelis asked carefully.

"For the moment I think you can choose where to travel," Marheh said. "I doubt we'll be closely observed yet. When we get closer you'd best be off *Day Bringer* though."

"I'll stay with you while I can then."

"Good. We can clear up here while Kel and Loc are getting ready. We'll be stopping again before long. The next symbol isn't far."

The next symbol, when they reached it, turned out to be an illusion. Kel, going very slowly past the place where they thought it would be, in Yareblis boat No. 3, felt nothing. Gelis, sheltered in *Day Bringer*'s saloon, fought against a limited return of her nightmare bird. Marheh, outside at the tiller, knew with most of her mind that her hands had not melted like hot wax and disappeared. Loc on boat No. 7 did not even realise they had reached the place.

Once they were all past and through bridge eight Kel pulled over to moor. Marheh had given him the Yareblis chart, since he was leading, but he knew they needed to consult. It was a surprise to discover that there had been an illusion and to realise that the Yareblis boats had not triggered it.

"I've been thinking," Marheh said when Kel had responded to her description of the illusion.

"Not again," he teased.

She gave him a little push.

"These boats need to be renamed. The Yareblis will know who should own *Boat 3* and *Boat 7* and they don't know you."

Kel nodded slowly.

"It wouldn't take long to paint the 3 into a B and I'm pretty sure the 7 could become an A without too much over painting. I could do it. This side now and the other side after the locks when the tow path changes sides."

He nodded again.

"It makes sense. Do you have the paint?"

"I've got white but no blue that would match what is there."

"Does it matter if we don't use blue? You'll have dark green, won't you? Using that would help the disguise. Obviously we are Yareblis from up north somewhere don't you think?"

She nodded.

"I'll get it – and we had better practise calling them *A* and *B*."

She was the best with a paint brush. Gelis found the paint while she pencilled in her alterations to the numbers then it was only a ten minute job to alter the numbers on the tow path side. When she had finished she stood back to examine her work.

"Not bad. It will be worth the trouble I think."

Kel nodded and took her paint brush and the turps to clean it.

"So, from now on, we have *Boat A* and *Boat B*," he said looking at the apprentices. "Okay."

* * * *

The locks were not far from where they had stopped and half way up the flight was another circle with a triangle in it.

"If that shows another booby trap," Kel said. "It will be interesting to discover whether the Yareblis boats are affected."

"Presumably they won't be," Marheh said. "After all they need to use the locks to get to Clanning. It's a bad place for a trap though."

"At least we know to be careful."

She nodded. Kel knew she was not good at careful and gave her a sympathetic smile. She raised her eyebrows and shrugged.

"What's the plan then?"

"We moor at the foot of the locks and take stock, walk up the flight listening. Then we work *Boat B* all the way up. Watching and listening all the time."

Marheh nodded. The listening would be important.

"You realise that *A* and *B* could probably both fit into the same lock," she said. "Perhaps we should abandon the charade until after the locks."

"Why don't we wait until we get there to decide?" Kel suggested.

"That would be best," Marheh agreed. "We could get a feel for whether we are already being watched."

They moved on then, in formation, *B*, *Day Bringer* and *A*. Marheh was trying to imagine how she might behave as a prisoner. Would she be controlled? Would she be physically constrained? They were not comfortable thoughts, but necessary if she was to be convincing. Gelis sensed her preoccupation and refrained from speech for the most part.

Then came the locks. There were three fairly close together. The land around was not particularly hospitable, especially on the northern side where the scars from the years of mining still remained. Looking and listening did not reveal any sense of a Yareblis presence so it seemed sensible to work *A* and *B* through together.

The afternoon was already well on. They would be pushing to get all three boats to the top before evening especially as they needed to investigate very carefully around the second lock where the chart showed the Yareblis symbol.

A small disagreement between Marheh and Kel was settled when Marheh pointed out that the Yareblis boats were unlikely to be in any danger and they could listen just as well while they were working them up the flight. Then there was the question of who would walk and who would drive, and whether listening would be best done from within a boat in a lock or from the lock side. Kel wanted to be taking the most risk. Marheh wanted to look and listen from within lock two. She didn't care about the other two.

"You just want a turn of steering a Yareblis boat," Kel teased her, giving way.

She put her nose in the air.

"Of course I do. I can't have my apprentice being one up on me."

All went well getting *A* and *B* up the flight. Marheh's listening warned her of danger but told her nothing specific, so when it came time for *Day Bringer* to ascend she would not let Gelis stay on board. She would have liked her to stay away from the lock workings too, but understood she would rebel if she insisted. It seemed likely that the boat would be the focus of the trap, if there was one, but it could be the operators as it had been at the bridge.

Day Bringer crept into the bottom lock with Marheh hardly daring to breathe. Loc and Gelis closed the gates behind her and Kel slowly opened one of the top paddles. The lock proceeded to fill just as it ought and before long *Day Bringer* was up and out and making her careful way towards lock two. Marheh watched from her position at the tiller as Loc and Gelis ran ahead to open the paddles and empty the lock.

They were not racing to get it done, she was glad to see. There were so many possible pitfalls, chances for injury, at locks. They had opened the gates for her by the time she reached them and she took *Day Bringer* slowly in, every sense alert and watchful. When *Day Bringer*'s front fender was just touching the top gate, ready to slide up the smooth surface in the centre of the gate, they closed the gates behind her. Kel was at the top gate watching for her signal. So far so good.

She nodded and he began to let the water in. It seemed to be filling quite fast even though he had only opened one paddle. She was going up alright though, wasn't she?

"Drop the paddle!" she shouted suddenly.

Kel reacted immediately, letting the paddle down with a rush.

"She's caught on something," Marheh called. "Can you see it?"

Day Bringer's back deck was angled forward, the prow held down somehow. A minute more with water running in and she could have been swamped.

Marheh tried a little reverse, but *Day Bringer* would not leave the top gate. Kel came carefully around the gate beam to look over into the lock.

"It's a big hook. It must have been triggered by the paddle."

107

Marheh turned to where Loc and Gelis still stood on opposite sides of the lock beside the bottom gates.

"We'll have to let some water out again," she called. "Gelis, can you open your paddle, just a little."

Slowly, as the water began to run out, *Day Bringer* levelled again, but the hook still held her in place against the top gate. Kel was in the best position to see how the prow was held.

"I think you'll have to keep her up to the top gate, tight as you can, and hope she'll slide down and out of the hook if we let more water out."

Marheh nodded. That made sense. She could trust Kel's judgement.

She inched the throttle down so that *Day Bringer* pressed against the gate. For a moment or two it seemed as if the hook would hold her. The back deck had begun to tilt a little the opposite way, but then her weight became too much for the hook and she slid down with a splash. Marheh immediately throttled back then looked up at Kel to share her relief.

Now it would be a question of keeping *Day Bringer* from touching either gate as they let the lock fill again. She had about a foot at each end if she kept her centred. It was not completely straightforward. The water running in again meant she needed to be constantly adjusting the throttle, but Kel was both careful and watchful and eventually the lock filled. *Day Bringer* rose smoothly with the water until the gate could be opened and she was released.

The two apprentices had gone to prepare the third lock once it was clear that they were no longer needed at the second so all was ready for Marheh to steer straight in. This time everything worked as it should and ten minutes later she was up and out and mooring in the space they had left between boats *B* and *A*.

"We won't go any further today," Kel said, seeing the tension drain out of her.

She nodded, suddenly weary.

"You'll come and eat on *Day Bringer*?" she said, holding herself together enough to make the invitation.

"Yes, but…" Kel began.

"Loc and I have planned the menu," Gelis interrupted. "We are going to cook."

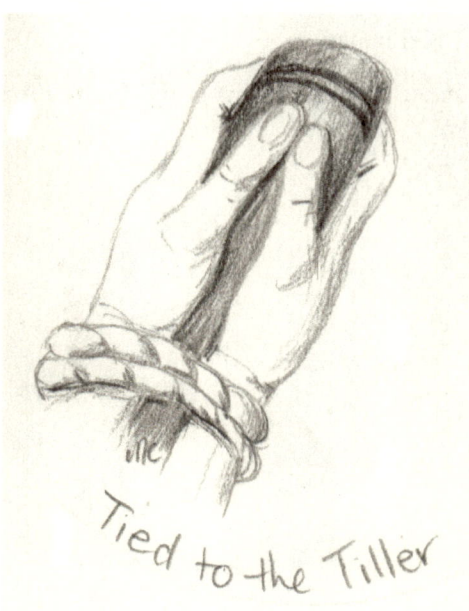

Tied to the Tiller

CHAPTER NINE

A meal, a discussion about the way forward, time to sing together and finally bed. Tomorrow the charade would begin in earnest.

Marheh had been so tired she fell into sleep the moment her head reached the pillow but she woke very early. The sky showed only the merest hint of colour on the eastern horizon and the dawn chorus had not begun although one lone songster was warbling a greeting to the day.

"All very well for you," she addressed the bird.

She was not looking forward to the day ahead. A day's journey would see them very close to Clanning although there was a new Yareblis symbol along the way that might hold them up for a while. She was going to play the prisoner. No matter that it had been her suggestion and that she still believed it to be the best way to get close to their enemies, the idea was confronting. She closed her eyes and reached for her portal to the soul song. There was time yet.

Kel had found sleep elusive. The bed on *Boat A* was all wrong, too short and too soft. He couldn't help being worried for Marheh. He had been called upon in the past when Yareblis action had threatened to get the better of her. This charade on which they were to embark would bring back events she would rather not remember. She was planning to act as if she had been controlled. There was a time, once, when she really had been. If he couldn't sleep he could sing and wrap her in light and love.

Loc found himself thinking over the events of the day as he lay waiting for sleep on *Boat B*. Gelis had been good to work with. Even though she had only been apprenticed such a short time she had understood what was needed at the locks. She obviously admired and respected her mentor too. It had been a good day, the challenge of the different boat, the locks and the threat to *Day Bringer* and then the time cooking with Gelis and the meal for which Marheh and Kel had been grateful and said so.

Gelis took out her journal when she found herself with too much to think about. Setting down her thoughts would settle her she knew.

Today was a very long day, she began. *Lots has happened. We started out very early. I was only half awake. We stopped hear the bridge where there was a symbol on the chart. It turned out to be a booby trap and Kel might have been badly hurt if Marheh hadn't called to him. She is a bit on edge at the moment I think. There was a horrible notice, like a wanted poster, on one of the Yareblis boats. It really upset her, though she tried not to show it. She is so brave. In the morning, when we set off again, she is going to pretend to be our prisoner and I'm sure she is uneasy about it.*

I enjoyed the walk with Kel and Loc when we went back to get a couple of the Yareblis boats. Loc was telling me about some of the places he has been with Kel and Kel talked a bit about Marheh and the things she has done. Kel and I came back together on Boat A and we talked then too, about what we are doing and how Loc and I might be able to help. It's often hard to remember that Marheh is seventy and Kel six years older. They seem so young and alive. I decided that our most useful contribution would be cooking the meals. Tonight we made a casserole with vegetables and a tin of fish.

She put down her pen and sighed. Cooking seemed very trivial compared with the actions Marheh and Kel could take, but it was appreciated. She got into bed and lay awake for a minute or two, thinking about Marheh and how much she admired her and wondering whether she would be sleeping on one of the Yareblis boats after the next night. Sleep took her before she found an answer to that question.

They gathered for breakfast on *Day Bringer*, but that was quickly over. Kel and Marheh went out to consider how best to proceed. Marheh had already changed the other numbers to letters now that the tow path had changed sides. *Day Bringer* was to be towed by *Boat B* but it might be important to be able to release her quickly. Marheh brought out the short, cut ends of *Day Bringer*'s lines, the ones she had kept after her moorings had been tampered with by the Yareblis in Deerford, and she and Kel roughly spliced a second loop on each. The result was two short lengths of rope with a loop at each end. *Day Bringer* would be towed on about five feet of line by *Boat B*. *Boat A* would act as an anchor if necessary, fastened to *Day Bringer*'s stern. Gelis and Loc would travel in *Boat B*, one to steer, one to watch. Kel would steer *Boat A*. Being an anchor required more expertise. The hulls of the Yareblis boats were much lighter that *Day Bringer* and would be easily damaged if *Day Bringer* slid into one or the other of them.

All was ready too soon for Marheh. She and Kel released *Day Bringer*'s mooring lines then stepped onto the back deck together. Carefully Kel bound Marheh's wrists to the tiller. He thought she looked pale.

"Poor little prisoner," he said lightly and kissed her.

Her eyes flashed and her chin went up and he smiled at the emergence of Marheh the Great.

"Ready?"

She nodded.

A few minutes later they were away, travelling slowly, taking time to get used to the way the boats moved together.

For a time all Marheh could manage was her breath, in, out, slow and deep, calming. She had not realised how this pretence would affect her. When she had steadied herself she began to listen, not relinquishing herself entirely to the soul song, but holding her portal ahead of her and allowing its light to fall on the landscape. This section had not changed much in all the years since she had last travelled this way. No real sign of habitation, just dry looking fields with a few sheep or cattle or a poor crop emerging. It was a grey, dreary place, seen in the light of her candle flame, but held no particular threat that she could detect.

Kel's mind reached her then, full of concern for her. She could reassure him now. The fleeting contact warmed and comforted her. Whatever the day held he was with her. The yet unknown Yareblis symbol was opposite the bridge to the village of Ponder. Forty years ago she had visited Ponder and made friends with two sisters who had helped her evade Yareblis pursuit. She had visited them with Nemle whenever they had the Clanning Branch included in their route but that was many years ago now. The sisters had been closer to Nemle's age than her own. Would she even recognise Ponder now? Would it have spread towards the water road? It had been useful to the Yareblis in the past. Was it still a place where they found support? There was not much point in asking herself all these questions to which she had no answers, but the slow procession left her with little to do but think. Occasionally a sharper bend, a longer curve in the water road, required her to move the tiller to help *Day Bringer* follow *Boat B*, but otherwise she had too much time and too little knowledge to feel she was using it productively.

Would the Yareblis boats that Gelis had seen leaving have gone all the way to Clanning? If they had, where would they have moored? The Clanning Branch ended at what had been the local pond. Boats could turn there and make their way back to the covered mooring where the old coal boats had been loaded. That had been Silberay built, but perhaps the Yareblis had taken it for their own. There were not many other possible moorings in Clanning itself. The water road there was too narrow.

Perhaps they would discover the boats along the way, with or without their owners. All she wanted was to get close enough to remove the water dimension from those remaining Yareblis who might otherwise continue in their attempt to harvest Silberay minds. If the Yareblis became aware of her she would be attacked, perhaps even broken. It was why she had suggested this pretence. If they thought her controlled they would have other plans for her. The realisation caused her a brief shudder.

Kel had been so gentle and careful tying her wrists, but the position was not natural and she was beginning to feel a degree of strain. A break for the toilet would make her feel more comfortable too but they had not planned to stop for a while yet. She took herself back to her listening. It was the most useful thing she could do and would make the time pass.

On *Boat B*, Loc was very conscious of his responsibility to keep everything moving steadily. The white boat handled very differently with *Day Bringer*'s solid weight dragging behind. He was glad of Gelis, standing beside him in the cockpit but looking back, checking distances. For the most part there were no particular challenges but a bend close to a bridge needed extra care to make sure *Day Bringer* was not pulled around too sharply.

Although she said very little he was aware that Gelis was also watching Marheh, what she could see of her, above the length of *Day Bringer*'s roof. He was not surprised that she was concerned for her.

"It must be frightening," he said, when he had begun to feel on top of his steering. "Even pretending."

Gelis nodded.

"Sometimes I wonder whether I should be frightened, but I don't know enough."

Loc smiled at that.

"You've experienced a little of what the Yareblis can do," he said. "So have I, but mentors promise to give their minds or even their lives for us if necessary. Kel and Marheh will keep us safe."

"I don't want to be kept safe if it costs Marheh her mind," Gelis said after a long pause. "I want to be in there fighting too."

"Well you have been, haven't you?"

Silence reigned for a while before Loc spoke again.

"We planned a stop after the next bridge," he said and Gelis could hear a degree of tension in his voice. "It's going to be tricky. Can you be ready to fend off if *Day Bringer* gets too close?"

Mooring went smoothly. Kel put *Boat A* into reverse to hold *Day Bringer* back a little so no fending off was necessary. As soon as they were all secured he went to release Marheh.

He stood back from her once her wrists were free and she walked stiffly to the back door but made a bolt for the bathroom once she was down the steps. Kel followed her as far as the back cabin and was waiting to give her a hug when she emerged.

"Are you alright?" he asked, holding her away so he could see her face.

She nodded.

"I know now that we are observed," she said. "I didn't see anyone one, but I was attacked. It was not strong and I slapped it down by pretending to be you." She gave him a little grin and growled "Get away, she's mine."

Kel gave a short laugh.

"You, pretending to be controlled, pretending to be me, pretending to be Yareblis!"

"All of that. But I think you are going to have to actually place a control. Anyone experienced would recognise that I don't have one."

He nodded. It made sense and they had challenged each other so often for practice that he knew how to do it without hurting her as long as she was willing.

"Go on," she said as he hesitated. "I trust you."

His mind approached hers and was welcomed. He entered and spoke then departed leaving behind the words of command. He had been careful and gentle and without her long experience and skilled practice she would not have recognised the invasion.

"Go on," she said again. "You'd better test it."

A little smile, a gentle nudge and she found herself turning on the spot. Then he took her in his arms again. A few minutes later they moved through to the saloon for food.

"Gelis looks too light hearted to be Yareblis," Marheh said, cutting cheese for her slice of bread. "I'll see if she has some darker clothes before we go on. You could take them to her and suggest she dampen down her curls. I'm worried for her she's so inexperienced."

Kel nodded.

"I'm a bit concerned for Loc too," he said. "But they won't let us leave them behind and maybe they wouldn't be any safer if we did."

The brief meal was soon over. Marheh found jeans to replace Gelis' shorts and a darker, long sleeved top.

"She won't want to wear these in this nice weather," she said. "So impress upon her that it is part of the pretence."

He took the things and put them on *Day Bringer*'s roof while he tied Marheh's wrists again. No kiss this time in case they were observed but Marheh spoke his name quietly as he turned to leave her.

"If you should need to prove that you have me controlled, that you are Yareblis, you mustn't hesitate, for all our sakes."

He turned back.

"Just what are you planning?" he asked in a fierce whisper.

She didn't answer and he had no time to press her. Loc had started the engine on *Boat B*. Kel grabbed the clothes for Gelis and hurried to give them to her before loosening the single line that held *Day Bringer* and returning to *Boat A*.

Kel's question lingered with Marheh as they moved off. What was she planning? The answer might be to get as close to Yareblis headquarters as she could without endangering her companions. But she could not do that without her companions who did not want to be kept from danger if they could help her. She needed to remember that. This was no time to act independently, better to think constructively about what she might encounter.

In the cockpit of *Boat A* Kel could see her well. The forward section of the white boat was quite short and so was the line between the boats. She stood squarely, feet a little apart, back straight, looking forward, but, having her wrists bound to the tiller forced her to turn a little towards him instead of facing straight ahead. He had hated tying her and tried to argue that it was unnecessary since he was supposed to have controlled her, but saw the logic of having an outward sign.

Briefly he sent his mind to hers, a small message of care and affection. They would be approaching the bridge to Ponder very soon and he remembered waiting for her there on *Day Bringer* when they were both still apprentices. Then she had been keeping out of

116

sight of men in uniform pursuing her. She had swum towards *Day Bringer* from the bridge ahead. She had been so beautiful, standing on the back deck in the moonlight, naked and dripping wet, but she seemed to him to be no less beautiful now. True, her hair was mostly grey and there were lines on her forehead and around her eyes, but her smile was still a gift and the shining of her soul song seemed to glow ever more strongly within her.

She could still be exasperatingly stubborn at times, but not as convinced that she knew best as she had been fifty years ago when they first met.

Ahead Loc had slowed *Boat B*. Kel gave a little burst of reverse to slow *Day Bringer* then looked ahead. *Boat B* was barely twenty yards from the bridge to Ponder, but they did not need to be through the bridge to see what the Yareblis symbol might mean. An area of land was enclosed by a high cyclone fence. There was a very ordinary looking shed at the end furthest from the water road and two cars were parked, one next to the shed and the other further along the fence. Also enclosed was an expanse of water with almost empty gantries running out from the banks. One solitary white boat floated there.

Boat B was under the bridge and Kel turned his attention there, anxious in case the symbol meant more than an empty marina. *Boat B* would be unlikely to be troubled but *Day Bringer* might trigger some new trap. What if there was something like the brick that had fallen? Marheh couldn't dodge. He wanted to call to Loc to stop, but it was already too late. *Day Bringer*'s prow slipped under the arch and he saw the shadow pass across her roof until it reached Marheh, so close to him, but impossibly far if she was at risk. He held his breath but then she was safely through and he had only to attend to his own steering.

Beyond the bridge he had time to take in the entrance to the Yareblis marina, blocked by a narrow drawbridge and to see, on the opposite bank, how Ponder had expanded towards the water road in a clutter of roof tops and boxlike houses. It puzzled him that there were so few boats moored, but of course they had been mostly left behind after Marheh had disabled their owners. The ones that Gelis had seen leaving had perhaps gone closer to Clanning.

On *Boat B*, Loc was feeling his responsibility. He had never travelled the Clanning branch and never towed another boat. The white boat handled very differently to *Storm Cloud*. They would not get all the way to Clanning today, but perhaps that wouldn't matter. Kel had taken a moment to assure him that he was managing well when he came with the clothes for Gelis. He'd even left it to him to decide when and where they would stop next.

Gelis emerged from below, having changed, rather reluctantly into the clothes Kel had brought.

"Do I look more like a Yareblis?" she asked.

Loc grinned.

"I suppose so. What does a Yareblis look like really?"

Gelis thought about the few she had met.

"They are very serious," she said. "And, and self important. I don't think they could ever be casual and light hearted, so I can see why Marheh wanted me to change."

Loc nodded.

"You've probably met more of them than I have, going to work at that club. Were you scared?"

"I was at first, but the work was pretty boring."

She moved to the stern to look over to *Day Bringer* and Marheh, then turned back to Loc.

"I hate that Marheh is doing this. She looks so remote. I can't see her very well, but she is very still and her face is, is sort of blank."

"She'll be listening or singing I expect." Loc glanced at Gelis. "I can understand you being worried but she is very strong and she knows what she is doing. She chose this way."

"I admire her so much and she has been really good to me but I don't feel as if I know her very well."

Loc thought for a few moments.

"In some ways I don't think many of the Silberay know her well, only Kel and her Uncle Jik and perhaps Dom who was Jik's apprentice and Bixa, Jik's soul friend. Something happened when she was quite young that coloured her relationship with the Silberay for a long time Kel told me."

Gelis looked at him, a question on her face, but he shook his head.

"I don't know any more than that."

Gelis sighed.

"I wish…"

Loc waited, but she didn't articulate her wish.

"After my second Gathering *Storm Cloud* and *Day Bringer* had intersecting routes," he said. "There was a problem in one of the really remote villages. The mentors thought it needed addressing and that one alone would be at risk. I was not far enough along to be able to help much. *Storm Cloud* went one way and *Day Bringer* another but we met at Fulbridge. It is nearly as far as you can go on the water road and it took forever to get there. We weren't travelling fast. The job wasn't urgent they didn't think and fast is not the Silberay way so autumn was well on by the time we met up. Already it was bitterly cold. I can't imagine what the place would have been like in winter. *Day Bringer* was already there at the mooring when we arrived but Marheh had gone off somewhere, we thought probably into the village for provisions. We weren't worried at first, but she wasn't back by tea time. Kel went to see if she had left any clues on *Day Bringer*, but there was nothing. I could tell he was worried though he tried to hide it. Then she sent her mind to him. She was alright, but she wouldn't be back that night. Then she showed him a picture of the place where he was to go next morning to meet her.

It turned out she had been arrested by the village policeman and spent the night in the local lock up."

"But, couldn't she have… you know, done the mind thing to make him let her go?"

Loc nodded.

"That's one of the reasons why I'm telling you. It was a real lesson to me. She could have and the Silberay would not have blamed her but she chose not to because of the policeman. He had a Yareblis control that he was fighting as best he could without understanding what it was. She wanted to help him. She knew she could, but that would draw Yareblis attention to her."

"What happened?"

"She let him lock her up, thinking that perhaps a Yareblis would come to see who or what he had arrested. It would be a better outcome for the policeman and for the village if she could disable the Yareblis. That would undo the control the policeman was fighting and prevent it being replaced as well as change the power structure in the village."

Gelis looked again towards Marheh then back to Loc.

"And that is a bit like what she is doing now, isn't it?" she said.

"I suppose it is," Loc said.

"So it must have worked," Gelis said.

Loc nodded.

"The local magistrate was Yareblis. He came to see the prisoner quite late that night. Marheh disabled him and sent the water dimension to Kel to destroy. Kel told me as we were walking into the village the next morning. When he recognised that the place Marheh had shown him was the police station he made up a story about his wife being missing. The policeman was quite apologetic when we talked to him. Apparently the charge was vagrancy. Of course Marheh couldn't prove where she lived and she had not been carrying more than money for milk, so, he explained, he really had no choice but lock her up. He brought her out to us looking none the worse for her night in gaol and told Kel he should scold her for being so improvident. Kel nodded and signed the book for her."

Loc smiled.

"I remember she was quite indignant about that. 'As if I was a parcel,' she said. We stayed a few more days to be sure, but she had basically done what we were sent to do. All the Yareblis controls in the village disappeared once the magistrate was disabled and people had the freedom to care for each other and act like good neighbours again."

* * * *

Marheh had spent much of the journey listening or singing but both of these began to demand more of her than she had to give. Her song, which sometimes was able to sustain her, struggled to maintain itself in a setting of grey desolation and listening showed her more of the same. The strain of her pretence was wearing her down so that she knew she would need to rest for a little if she was to be fit for the job she had undertaken. The day's journey seemed to have gone on forever and she longed for it to stop so she could go below to eat and sleep. Was Loc planning to continue as long as he could see? Sunset was late this time of year. She wanted to reach Kel and beg for the journey to pause a little, but pride held her back. Along *Day Bringer*'s roof she could see Gelis looking back from *Boat B* and steeled herself to continue.

"Are we going to stop soon?" Gelis asked Loc. "I think Marheh has had enough."

"Has she let you know?"

"No, she wouldn't, but…"

"After the next bridge then," Loc suggested. "The water road is so straight here we shouldn't have trouble finding a long enough mooring."

The next bridge was in sight, just a dot in the distance. It seemed a long way off to Gelis but it was, at least, an end in view. She would have liked to ask if Loc had any more stories about Marheh but thought perhaps it might be better to ask Marheh herself to tell her things. That way she could choose what she wanted Gelis to know. Instead she asked Loc about himself.

"Have you been all over the water road?"

He shook his head.

"Not here, obviously, and not the southern route. Kel prefers the northern routes. They tend to be a bit more challenging I think."

"Do you have a favourite place?"

Again he shook his head.

"It's the journey I like, moving from place to place, learning about the people, listening to the landscape."

"Marheh talks about listening, but I don't really understand it yet."

"You will, especially with Marheh as your teacher. I don't hear what she hears, or Kel, but I'm beginning to be able to recognise if a place is hurting or if it is content."

The bridge was closer now, bigger than a dot, but still quite far. Gelis longed to be able to tell Marheh that the day's ordeal was nearly over. She looked towards her, wishing she knew how to send her thoughts the way Marheh did, making a picture of the bridge in her mind and imagining she was showing it to Marheh.

It wouldn't work of course but there was no harm in trying.

Then, suddenly, she understood that something had reached her, for Marheh was there in her mind, just for a moment of thanks and affection. She closed her eyes the better to look inward to appreciate it then looked again towards Marheh. Her face was still blank as if she was controlled but Gelis knew that inwardly she had smiled, just for her.

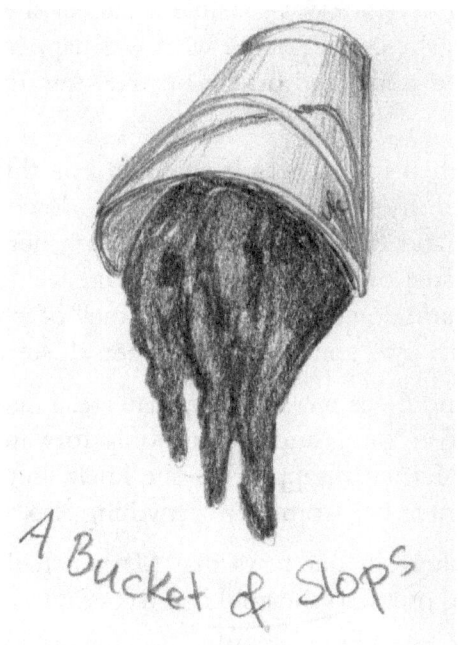

A Bucket & Slops

CHAPTER TEN

Boat B was still a couple of lengths from the bridge when two cars appeared, travelling fast towards them from the south. Marheh saw them and her heart sank. There seemed something deliberate about this approach. Not all the bridges they had passed beneath carried roads, some just carried footpaths or bridle paths, but there had been others where roads had crossed. Once there had been a cyclist, pedalling madly, oblivious of the water road. Once there had been a bus disappearing towards some distant village.

These cars seemed different. She could, at a pinch, have dealt with one, but she was very tired, so tired that even contacting Kel was an effort. He needed to practise controlling her, to show the Yareblis, if that is who they were, that he had her.

The cars raced up to the bridge. The leader stopped at the top of the arch, the other just behind it. Three men and a woman got out and stood looking towards the oncoming boats.

Marheh felt Kel's control acting to make her kneel and bow her head. Her hands, still bound to the tiller, reached up as if in supplication. Subservience was sensible whatever she felt inside. With her head lowered she could not see what was happening above her as *Day Bringer* passed under the bridge but Kel saw them lift a bucket onto the parapet.

Suddenly Marheh found herself engulfed in a thick, foul smelling liquid. It dripped from her hands and ran down her bent back, soaking her hair and her clothes. At least, with her head down, her face was largely free of it, although she could feel it trickling slowly around her chin and down her neck. The smell of it almost made her gag. She closed her eyes and tried to hold herself steady.

Ahead, Loc and Gelis were largely unaware. Loc was focusing on the possibility of mooring and looking only forward. Gelis, looking back, had seen Marheh disappear as she knelt, but the bulk of the bridge had prevented her from seeing anything else.

She was pouring out her fears that Marheh had perhaps fainted and urging Loc to moor so she could go to her.

"You can't," Loc told her. "She's supposed to be Kel's prisoner."

"But…"

"But nothing. Kel will take care of her if she needs it. Your job is to help me moor. Does it look as if Kel is through the bridge?"

She could see the top of *Boat A* over *Day Bringer*'s roof.

"A little further I think," she said, wanting to ignore his words, but knowing he was right.

Kel, wanting to reach Marheh's mind to assure himself that she was alright, had not been concentrating on what was happening ahead. When he did, it was too late to stop Loc from mooring. He was only just in time to reverse so that *Day Bringer* would not crash into *Boat B*.

Marheh felt his concern. Be Yareblis, she tried to tell him, sending him a couple of images of how he might. She felt him recoil. Don't be soft, use the opportunity, she sent him.

The four Yareblis had come down from the bridge when they realised the cavalcade was mooring up. One of the men took Kel's line as he came in, the other three went to stare at Marheh and mock.

"It's mine," Kel said, remembering how Marheh had repelled the earlier attack. "And mine the reward."

He tried to be coldly triumphant, if such a thing was possible.

The Yareblis backed a little and held up a placatory hand.

"Of course. Just want to see how you manage it."

"You will," Kel said, hating what he was about to do.

Reaching down into the back of *Boat A*, he pulled out a bucket and dipped it into the water road. I'm sorry Marheh, he wanted to say, but hardly dared even think it.

Do it.

It was Marheh in his mind. He sloshed the water over her. She continued to kneel with bowed head. He stepped up onto *Day Bringer* and reached across to the tiller. Fastidiously avoiding the filth that still lingered over Marheh and over *Day Bringer*'s back deck he untied her wrists. Stepping back to join the Yareblis he activated his control.

Slowly she got up from her knees, took two steps across *Day Bringer*'s deck and onto the gunnel, paused a moment, then stepped off into the water.

She would have had to do it anyway, she thought wryly, standing up to her arm pits in the cold. No way would she have gone below smelling the way she had.

She stood still for a moment then, as nothing further came from Kel, she decided to continue as if it had. Taking the biggest breath she could without it being obvious, she bent her knees and sank slowly down beneath the water. She remained submerged, letting her breath trickle out very slowly, until she thought her lungs would burst with the effort. Then she stood again, gasping, still facing the opposite bank.

Getting out would probably be easier on the offside where the ground sloped a little and there was the bridge to bring her back. Moving steadily, as if controlled, she began to wade across the narrow strip of water. She would have liked to be able to just walk out, but the bank was quite steep and she needed her hands and arms to help her. She could sense Kel's concern for her now and sent him the image of her grin. Almost she was enjoying herself fooling the

Yareblis. Their next encounters she would be rested and able to act against them.

Once out of the water, she continued to walk, deliberately taking the most direct route to the bridge although it meant stepping over a small bush and pushing into the lower branches of a spindly tree. She remembered how it had been the time she had really been controlled by a Yareblis, how inexorably she had been propelled to where he wanted her and tried to replicate the feeling. She reached the bridge with all eyes on her. As she began to cross she glimpsed Gelis' anxious face.

Stay hidden, pretend, she sent, suddenly afraid that she would reveal herself.

Up and over the bridge she walked, squeezing past the Yareblis cars, leaving smears of muddy water on their polished sides. Without looking at any of them she walked along the tow path past *Boat A* and onto *Day Bringer* again. Then, slowly and deliberately, she divested herself of all her wet and dirty clothes. She paused for a moment or two, a slim, pale statue, then stepped to the back door and down into the cabin.

Kel hardly knew whether to admire her audacity or shake her for the series of frights she had given him. He mustn't waste what she had done though.

Marheh, sitting on the seat of the toilet undoing her plait, heard him dictating to the Yareblis.

"As you see, I have it under full control."

His voice sounded insufferably self important and Marheh couldn't help grinning a little.

"There will be an additional demonstration when we arrive at Clanning."

There were admiring murmurs from the Yareblis.

"You had best go and warn them to expect us," he went on, and now she heard condescension. "I will bring it along in my own time."

More murmurs and the sound of footsteps followed by the slam of car doors and the revving of engines.

"Just you wait!"

Kel's admonition reached her mind and she sent him back the image of a rather rude gesture. She heard him chuckle as he walked past to confer with Loc. They would be best to moor as far away from bridges as possible.

The memory of an earlier time came back to her, she and Kel on *Day Bringer* making their way to Clanning, planning to moor when the bridge behind them disappeared.

As soon as they were underway she would shower and wash her hair. The sound of the pump would be muffled by the engine noise from the other boats. The smell of what they had tipped over her still lingered and washing off the water road was advisable too. If she was careful she wouldn't use too much of their water. Then she would put herself to bed for a while. The Yareblis would hardly question now and she need not be on show, at least for the rest of today.

When she awoke it was nearly dark. They had moored and the smell of cooking drifted into her cabin. She sighed and stretched and realised that she was hungry. No point in getting dressed, especially since the only wearable trousers she had left were those she kept for best. The others wouldn't mind if she joined them in her nightdress, she thought, pulling it over her head. She pushed her feet into slippers and her arms into the sleeves of her dressing gown. When she emerged into the saloon she was still tying the belt around her waist.

The others were all there. Gelis and Loc were in the galley and Kel resting in the armchair. All three heads turned towards her and unexpectedly she felt herself blushing.

"You'd best come over here so I can tell you what I think of your behaviour," Kel said with mock ferocity.

Somehow that made everything alright.

She could laugh then and say demurely "But I was controlled!"

He stood up so she could have the armchair but she pushed him back and took her place on the footstool.

Gelis and Loc busied themselves tactfully with unnecessary supper preparations and tried not to listen.

"You're a wanton hussy," Kel said softly, taking one of her hands and playing with her fingers.

Marheh grinned.

"I know! Such fun! I convinced them didn't I?"

He looked at her and saw that something had sparked within her that had been absent ever since Deerford.

"I think you've been enjoying yourself. You look as if you're ready to respond to any challenge now."

She put her free hand over his.

"I was in a way, enjoying myself, not that ghastly smell, but it was very freeing, pretending to be controlled and knowing they were fooled has built my courage. I couldn't have tackled all four of them then, but at the moment I feel strong enough for anything."

He stood up and lifted her to her feet.

"Supper's ready," he said. "We'll plan later."

It felt safe and enclosed on *Day Bringer*. The lamps were lit and the curtains drawn, there was warmth from the stove and the smell of food, and, best of all, there was the warmth of love and affection from her companions.

Kel told her that Loc had washed down *Day Bringer's* back deck and Gelis had rinsed out her wet clothes.

"First in the water road, and then in the shower water, which we assumed you had left for that purpose," he said.

"I did," she said. "But I didn't expect you to do it. I'm very grateful." She smiled at Gelis "And grateful that you managed to keep up the pretence."

"Loc stopped me when I wanted to go to you," Gelis said. "I wasn't thinking straight."

"Both of you have done very well."

She looked impishly at Kel.

"Unlike him. I even had to control myself!"

"Watch yourself," he growled. "That control is still in place."

"I'm really scared," she said, laughing at him.

"So you should be."

They lingered over the meal, not wanting to address the more sober issue of planning their next step, but at length the food was eaten, the dishes done and they could make no more excuses.

"When would you prefer to reach Clanning?" Kel asked Marheh. "I tried to give the impression that I was above hurrying so I don't think an extra day or even two would matter." He leered at her. "Obviously I will want time to enjoy my power over you."

"Obviously," Marheh agreed, raising her eyebrows and glancing sideways at him across the table.

Gelis, sitting next to him, caught the look and gave a little giggle.

"This is supposed to be a sensible discussion," Marheh said severely, then spoilt the effect by smirking at Gelis who giggled again.

Kel laughed.

"I suppose I asked for that. I'm sorry. What is Madam's sensible answer to the sensible part of my remark?"

"Madam's sensible answer is that I don't mind if we wait a day, or even two, but I would like to arrive late at night or in the very early morning." She paused then continued without the bantering tone. "It worked well, disabling them while they slept. If I could do that again they might not realise that your prisoner was not controlled until it was too late."

"But could you get near enough to find them?" Kel asked. "We don't know how many there are either."

Loc and Gelis looked at each other then Loc spoke.

"Gelis and I had time to think while we were going along and we wondered whether it would be helpful if we walked ahead into Clanning and took a look at some of those places marked on the chart. You've not made much use of us up to now, but we want to help and Gelis would recognise some of them from her time working at the club."

"And they would recognise her," Marheh said sharply, unwilling to put her apprentice at risk.

"I don't think so," Gelis said. "Not if I tied my hair up and wore a dress and perhaps a sunhat. None of them ever really looked at me. I was too far beneath them."

"Not that red dress," Marheh said. "And do you even own a sunhat?"

"My mother insisted I have one," Gelis said grinning. "I just haven't worn it yet."

Gelis' mother was a red herring Marheh didn't want to pursue just now. If possible their route should include a visit to Gelis' family. It was important she kept in touch with them, but not until this business was behind them.

"Any way," Gelis went on. "They didn't suspect I was spying on them then, why should they now? If I see one I could be all upset that my job had disappeared and I hadn't been paid."

"If you see one you'll keep your head down, your hat on and point him out to Loc," Marheh said severely. "He can follow up. They don't know him."

"They might," Kel said. "The ones that brought us the food each day had time to notice."

Marheh looked around the table at them all.

"I don't think I'm cut out for a mentor," she said crossly. "How can I keep you safe of you go off on your own?"

There was a moment of surprised silence.

"Alright," she added. "You don't have to answer. I'm just being difficult. Of course you can go. It will be very helpful if you can pinpoint a few places for me."

Gelis and Loc looked at each other then smiled at Marheh. Kel, watching, saw her recognise that they were being particularly tactful and kind and waited for the explosion. It didn't come. She looked at him and made a face.

"Am I being the kind of old woman that needs to be humoured?"

He shook his head and was about to speak when Gelis jumped in.

"You'll never be an old woman. You're the best mentor. We only want to be useful, not just baggage to be lugged around."

Another silence.

"You are useful, both of you," Marheh said. "I apologise if I've made you feel like baggage." She took a deep breath. "Shall we get out the chart and plan your walk to Clanning?"

They spent time with the chart and the Yareblis map of Clanning as well as singing together before Loc and Kel went off to the other boats to sleep. Marheh banked the fire and was about to turn off the light in the saloon when she realised that Gelis was still hovering. She looked at her and smiled, a question in her eyes. Gelis took a step towards her then another. Marheh held out her arms and next moment they were hugging each other.

"Best if you go off to bed. You've an early start tomorrow," Marheh said, releasing her. "Sleep well."

"You too."

Easier to say than to do, Marheh thought, hanging up her dressing gown and turning back the covers. The day had held so many challenges and she had dealt with some better than others. She felt confident in the way she had dealt with the Yareblis, but the business of being a mentor was a continual challenge that she was not handling well. Thank goodness Gelis seemed willing to forgive her. She put out the light and opened her curtains. Had Nemle felt this way? She must have of course. There had been times when she had apologised, but the young Marheh had been arrogant and unforgiving, especially at first. She opened the door to the well deck and stood for a moment looking out at the starry night. Thoughts of Nemle, her own loving mentor, were both comfort and challenge.

"I'll keep trying," she promised then closed the door and put herself to bed.

* * * *

The morning when it came was bright and clear. A light breeze moved amongst the tall grasses and weedy plants that grew on the bank opposite and lifted little dust eddies amongst the rocks on the ground beside them. Nothing much had changed here in the thirty or so years since she had last travelled the Clanning Branch. There would be changes in Clanning though, bound to be, nothing stood still for thirty years except in fairy tales.

She got up and pulled on her dressing gown wondering whether her trousers would be dry enough to wear. Gelis had hung them in the engine room, but since they had not been using the engine that would not be as warm as usual.

Nowhere near dry enough was the answer. Never mind, Gelis would need a good breakfast. She could start the porridge without dressing and think about options later when she and Loc had gone.

The porridge was cooked and the kettle boiled when Gelis appeared. She had scraped her hair back off her face and into an elastic band on the nape of her neck. Her dress was a plain blue shift, knee length with short, set in sleeves. Marheh nodded her approval.

"It's a nice dress, but it doesn't shout like the red one."

Gelis laughed.

"It has useful pockets too. Loc is going to take a back pack but I won't need to unless you want me to shop."

Marheh shook her head.

"Just what we discussed last night and one pack should hold that."

Kel and Loc appeared then ready to join them for breakfast. Marheh welcomed them and apologised for her attire.

"Yesterday's clothes are not dry and I haven't many other options."

"It doesn't matter," Kel said easily. "You and I can relax today."

Breakfast was soon over and Gelis and Loc ready to depart. Marheh gave them each a hug but managed to restrain herself from loading them with advice. She and Kel watched from the well deck as they began the long walk that would take them to Clanning. Then, when the two figures were just dots in the distance, they went back into the galley to clear up the breakfast dishes.

* * * *

While Gelis and Loc were on the tow path there was no room to go side by side so the beginning of the journey was quite silent, but after about twenty minutes they came to the bridge where they were to leave the water road. Kel had shown them the route he had taken forty years ago, that circled Clanning to the north. It had been quiet and rural then, but they couldn't expect it to be the same now.

"It was a good idea of yours to make little drawings of bits of the map," Loc said, as Gelis stepped up next to him.

"I just remembered how conspicuous I always feel unfolding a map, especially in a town. It really marks you as a visitor."

Loc nodded.

"Making the sketch maps helps to learn the route too."

"Do you think we will find out anything useful?"

Loc shrugged.

"Hard to say. If we can confirm that the triangles on the map of Clanning show where there are Yareblis living that will be useful, but of course some of them might be ones that Marheh has disabled already."

Gelis nodded. She was still finding it difficult to understand exactly what disabling the Yareblis involved although she had seen the consequences of Marheh's action.

"Can you do it?" she asked Loc. "Enter someone's mind I mean."

"Not really. I'm fairly consistent communicating between me and Kel, but only if he initiates the contact. If I try to initiate it I need a pretty pressing reason and then I only succeed about half the time."

Gelis nodded.

"It helps, doesn't it, a pressing reason? I really wanted to tell Marheh that you were planning to stop after that bridge yesterday. I was so worried for her. I made a picture of the bridge and kept making it, and just when I had given up she smiled in my mind."

"That's pretty good for a first year. Mind you, you have a terrific mentor. Marheh is the best there is at the discipline of the mind."

Gelis nodded.

"I know I'm lucky. I think she's great."

The quiet country lane where they were walking stopped at a junction with a busier road. There were cars passing as they made the left turn that would take them towards Clanning and about one hundred yards on they reached a bus stop. They looked at each other and Loc went to study the information displayed on the back wall of the shelter.

"What do you think? Will we catch the bus? It goes to Clanning and there is one due in about fifteen minutes."

"It would give us more time to investigate," Gelis said. "I don't see why we shouldn't. It is probably less noticeable than walking."

She was enjoying spending time with Loc, someone close to her own age who didn't think she needed protecting.

"Marheh and Kel are so much older than we are," she said. "I suppose it is only natural that they think of us as children."

Loc nodded.

"Sometimes you can almost see them trying not to. The trouble is they know so much more than we do about the kinds of dangers we might face."

"This doesn't feel dangerous, but maybe that is ignorance talking."

Loc laughed.

"If that is the case then I am ignorant too."

They had time to chat for a few more minutes before the bus came and carried them expeditiously into the centre of Clanning. After a fifteen minute ride they alighted outside the town hall. They drifted away from the half dozen other passengers and looked about them.

"Shall we wander about a bit and get our bearings," Loc suggested.

"Perhaps we could find somewhere for a cup of coffee while we check the map."

* * * *

Marheh and Kel took about half an hour to finish the dishes and the clearing up.

"I'd really like to go for a walk," Marheh said, looking out wistfully at the bright day. "I suppose it wouldn't be sensible."

"Probably not," Kel agreed.

"You could practise controlling me."

"Have you dancing along the tow path in your night dress, or better yet in your birthday suit?" Kel teased.

She laughed.

"Perhaps not. Do you think Gelis and Loc were very shocked by what I did?"

"They watched you in the water and coming across the bridge but I don't think they could see the climax from where they were. You were pretty much hidden behind *Day Bringer*. Why? Is it worrying you?"

She thought for a moment.

"I suppose I'm a bit embarrassed in retrospect. It wasn't proper mentor behaviour."

"Rubbish. You did what needed doing."

He gave her a hug.

"The Yareblis were convinced you were under my control and that was important to safeguard us all. Now, what are we going to do with the day? Do you want to sleep, or sing or practice or play with your clay?"

"Not sleep," she said. "Let's practice. It's been ages, and then sing, but I'd better get dressed first."

* * * *

Gelis and Loc found the centre of Clanning a rather inhospitable place but they did manage to acquire a drink that was supposed to be coffee in a down at heel little café tucked between an empty shop front that appeared to have been a green grocery in a past life and a butcher's rather nasty window display. There was no one else in the café, which made them feel rather conspicuous, but they took out the bits of paper with their notes and conferred quietly, confident that they would not be overheard.

"It isn't a very nice town, is it?" Gelis said. "Do you think the Yareblis have made it this way?"

"It will be their influence I expect. People lose heart when they feel powerless and the Yareblis want them to feel that way so they can build their power and control."

Gelis nodded.

"Maybe what we do will make a difference."

"What we do, and more especially what Marheh and Kel will do."

"With us helping," Gelis said. "So where will we go first?"

Now that they were actually in Clanning their task seemed more difficult than they expected.

"I'm wondering whether we should see if we can find the white boats, the ones you saw leaving. It would be useful to know whether they came all the way here."

"We would have to be careful. That's one thing we do have to avoid, revealing that we can see them, but it's a good idea." Gelis pointed to a place on the little sketch map she had in front of her. "We can't go into the old Silberay mooring without it being obvious, but Marheh thought we might be able to catch a glimpse from this bridge and that's not far from here."

"And we might go and find the pond. Didn't she say the Silberay used that for a turning place? Maybe they've taken that over like they did in Deerford."

They paid for their coffee and set out, back to the town hall to get their bearings and then down a short, narrow street, shaded by the shops on either side, and into a wider road with more important looking stores.

Grim looking shoppers went to and fro, in and out, and cars drove up and down with impatient beeping and revving if anyone dared to impede their progress by trying to park. At the bottom of the long hill the road turned to their left for fifty yards or so before turning back to the right. Across the road was a long, low building that looked like a warehouse.

"That will be the mooring I think," Gelis said quietly as they waited to cross the road.

Loc nodded.

A gap in the traffic gave them time to scamper across and continue towards the bridge which rose gently over the water road and then debouched into a residential area.

"Did you see anything?" Gelis asked once they had crossed and were strolling past a row of tall, narrow terrace houses.

"I think so, but I'm not really sure. I didn't want to make it obvious that I was looking, especially since I don't know what the bridge goes over for people who don't see the water road."

"We'd get a better view going the other way I think," Gelis said. "The way Marheh described it, it should be open on that side."

"We need to go back anyway if we're going to try to find some of the places with symbols. They were all on the other side of town."

So, after a short stroll beside the houses, they turned back and crossed the bridge again. This time they didn't need to turn around to see. There were three white boats under the canopy.

"They didn't all stay near the entrance then," Gelis commented. "Some must have continued on here. I'm sure I only saw two leaving the morning after Marheh had acted."

"Perhaps some of them were never in Deerford," Loc suggested.

Gelis nodded.

"I think we had better look at the pond, don't you?"

It was not far. They walked back beside the mooring and turned off the main street along a quieter road. A five minute walk and they were there. The pond had been tidied up since Marheh had turned *Day Bringer* there. The rushes and the ducks she had described were gone and the pond was edged with concrete except for a gap of about three yards between two buildings.

"Do you think people wonder why they can't walk all around it?" Gelis commented as they wandered onto the path that curved around the rest of it.

Loc shrugged. There were no boats to be seen and the edge where they stood appeared too shallow to accommodate any.

"I think it's deeper in the middle though," Loc said. "They would still need to use it to turn even though their boats are so much shorter."

"What will happen to *Day Bringer* if we bring her as far as this?"

"Marheh will manage somehow," Loc said. "I think we've seen enough here. We'd better keep moving and see what we can discover about the symbols."

It meant another hike back to the main road and up the hill. They didn't need to go back to the town hall, but kept walking north until the commercial district disappeared and they were once more on residential streets.

"What are we going to do when we find one? I don't suppose we should just go and knock on the door. What kind of excuse would we have for doing that?"

"Looking for someone perhaps," Loc suggested. "Someone who lives in the street but we've lost the number."

"Well we don't have the number, not really, but it means showing ourselves. Marheh didn't want us to do that in case we were recognised. What if I do the knocking? I can always ask about my pay if I'm spotted. You can hide and watch so if anything happens you will know."

"I don't see why you should do the difficult bit. What will Marheh say if you get into trouble?"

"Tell her you couldn't stop me." Gelis grinned at him. "You know it makes sense. If anyone recognises you they will also know you are Silberay. They don't know that I am."

The argument continued as they walked along counting off dwellings until they reached the vicinity where they thought the marked house might be. The street was very quiet and they had seen no one as they walked. They kept to the side opposite and separated once they thought they were close, Loc staying back. When Gelis crossed the road to visit the house they had decided might be the one indicated on their map he lingered beside a big street tree from where he could watch and be inconspicuous.

Gelis approached the house with a degree of trepidation she hoped Loc had not noticed. As she walked up the short path to the front door she tried to put everything out of her head except the story that she was visiting her friend Amelia.

The front door was sheltered by a small canopy and reached by two shallow steps. A knocker, in the shape of a man's head holding a ring in his mouth, was fastened in the centre of the door. Taking a deep breath she reached up and banged the ring against the man's chin, once, twice and then a third time. Then she waited.

Probably there would be no one home. It was the middle of the working week after all. Maybe they had settled on the wrong house and she would need to try again next door. Then she heard footsteps. The door opened and there stood the Odd Messenger.

He would be sure to recognise her. Forget about the mythical Amelia.

"Oh good," she said. "I was hoping I had the right house. I worked four whole days at that club and never got paid. Next day when I went everyone had gone. I don't suppose you can pay me, but you must know where I can find the person who can."

We walked together, side by side
Then caught a bus
Pleased to be trusted to help
The two of us.

We saw the homes of enemies,
Explored the town,
Found it rather bleak and sad,
Grey, perhaps, or brown.

We visited someone I worked with,
Got an address.
Information to help our mentors
Know, not guess.

Gelis

CHAPTER ELEVEN

Practising the discipline of the mind together was rather like playing, Marheh thought, readying herself to meet Kel's attack. Some time for play might not be a bad thing, given the stresses of the last few days.

She and Kel had been practising together ever since Kel's mentor Sul retired and when Nemle retired it had become an almost daily event until Kel became a mentor. He had needed to practise with his apprentice then and she had missed the regular contact. Then Kel had been imprisoned and she had lost him. She let him feel her happiness at having found him again. His mind answered hers with a sense of warmth which became amusement as he activated his control and she found herself balancing on one leg, like a stork, arms outstretched for balance.

"I forgot you already had an advantage," she said aloud.

"I thought perhaps you had," he teased, watching her struggle to put her foot down again.

She could always beat him if they started equal so they never did. Marheh usually handicapped herself by giving her mind some other task to accomplish while they fought. The multiplication table worked well, or singing her way through the Silberay song book.

"It's not often I can be one up on you," Kel said.

"What makes you think you are now?"

Marheh grinned at him as her mind grappled with the control, bound it and gave it back to him. She put her foot firmly back beside the other one and waited for his next move.

They were not often together in body during this practice. They did not need to be, but since they were, Kel was licensed to use his greater physical strength if he could. He could hear her singing the song with which the Silberay honoured those retiring, but she had changed the words. '*You are the old, our wisdom, our strength*', it should have been but she sang '*no wisdom, no strength*'. He would not let her distract him with her taunts. He focused, looking for the weakness in her shield that would let him replace his control. Her physical presence was distracting and he knew she was aware of it and using her knowledge. With the part of her mind that was not occupied with the words of her song she was attempting to build an illusion that would have him see her as Loc.

"Oh no you don't," he said into her mind.

Before she could stop him he had tipped her across his knees and landed a light smack on her rear. She laughed and slid onto the ground and for a moment he was persuaded he saw a sleek, black seal lounging at his feet. The surprise of it enabled her to sneak in a control that had him standing and turning round and round on the spot. Then, before he had time to focus, she spun another illusion, this time a sticky thread that bound him into a cocoon as he turned and turned.

"Serves you right."

She allowed him to stop turning so he could bring his mind to bear on the illusion.

"Enough?" she said aloud.

"Enough," he agreed.

They laughed, hugged and decided on sperit and perhaps a bite of lunch.

* * * *

Gelis looked at the Odd Messenger and waited. Would he accept her words? If he did, would he respond with any useful information or just fob her off? Was he one of the Yareblis Marheh had disabled? Could he control her? Would he wish to?

The Odd Messenger stood in the doorway without speaking. His position on the doorstep gave him height enough to look her in the eye.

"You must realise that I can't afford to work for nothing," Gelis said when the silence had gone on long enough.

"You for the kitchen," he said in his high voice, as he had done when she had first applied for the job at the club.

He held the door wider and gestured for her to enter.

"You for the kitchen."

"I don't want to come in," Gelis said firmly. "I just want the wages I'm owed, or at least to know where to go for them."

She couldn't quite decide whether the pressure she felt to enter was an attempt to control her, or simply her natural politeness making her feel guilty that she was not accepting his invitation. She remained where she was. Another long silence while they looked at each other.

"They'll have you yet," the Odd Messenger said, and Gelis remembered he had said it before.

"Try number eleven," he added. "Number eleven Westall Road."

He shut the door quickly then but not before Gelis had glimpsed his look of sly satisfaction.

"Eleven Westall Road."

She murmured the address to herself as she returned to the street and began to walk back the way she had come, thinking it would be better if Loc did not have to pass the house to follow her. She was pleased with her discovery, knowing it would help Marheh when it came time for her to act.

Loc crossed the road to join her after she had passed about half a dozen houses.

"I don't think we need to go to the address," he said, when she had reported her findings.

"Probably best if we don't," Gelis agreed. "I got the impression that he wanted me to."

"So now what?"

"We should look at the map again I think and see if Westall Road is near here and if there are any other places with symbols."

There was a corner ahead and they waited until they reached and turned into it before taking out the sketch maps they had made. Westall Road was quite close and they saw where they had copied the Yareblis symbol half way along.

"And number seven Baggers Lane is not far either," Gelis pointed out. "But we don't need to go there. We know the one who lives there is already disabled."

"I think we've done enough," Loc said. "We've confirmed the meaning of the symbol and we've seen the Yareblis boats. Any more might draw attention we don't need."

Gelis nodded slowly. She was not entirely convinced, but the day was getting on and she had no concrete suggestion for further action.

"We might as well do that bit of shopping anyway," she said. "Then it is out of the way if we think of anything else."

They found a small local supermarket and were wandering the aisles looking for the items on their list when Loc caught sight of another shopper and pulled Gelis into a different aisle.

"See if you recognise her? I think she might be the woman who came to see Marheh controlled."

Gelis sauntered casually past the end of the aisle and nodded.

"We should follow her if we can. We know she hasn't been disabled," Loc said when they were together again.

It made sense. Loc took their purchases to the cashier and Gelis drifted outside and stood looking at the shop window and pretending to read the few advertisements. She could see the woman, on and off, as she passed up and down. It was definitely the woman who had arrived with the three men at the bridge. She was glad now that she had followed Loc's advice and stayed in the shadow of the boat's canopy. The woman was very unlikely to have had view of her.

Loc was taking his time arranging his purchases carefully in his backpack but the woman still had not approached the cashier. Gelis saw him hoist the pack onto his back and leave the shop, passing her without any acknowledgement of her presence and walking a little way away before pausing and looking back. Gelis thought how useful it would be if she could communicate with her mind the way Marheh did. She dared not signal in case the woman emerged and caught her at it. She was at the cash register now though so it would not be long before she came out. Which way would she turn? Would she be on foot or in one of the cars parked on the other side of the road?

As if he had caught her thought, Loc crossed and stood half hidden beside a lamppost. If she was in a car they would not be able to follow, but at least they could get a general direction and a number plate for future recognition.

A moment later the woman swept out. She carried a handbag but no shopping and stepped out smartly, turning away from Gelis in the direction Loc had taken. She saw Loc register this and begin to walk along the street, keeping a little ahead. She would hardly suspect him of following from in front of her. If she went into one of the houses or turned a corner Gelis would see, and then Loc would come after.

She waited until the woman was well ahead and began to walk in the same direction.

* * * *

Marheh put down her empty mug and looked across the table at Kel.

"I wish…" she began.

"What's the matter?" he asked.

"I keep thinking I should be with Gelis. What if something goes wrong?"

"Loc would communicate with me," Kel said. "He knows enough for that, but they are both sensible, they won't take unnecessary risks."

Marheh sighed.

"I just feel as if I'm failing Gelis. I've hardly begun to teach her."

"I thought you told me she sent you a picture of the bridge where the Yareblis were. That's very promising for someone so new to it. You can't expect her to be like you were."

"No, she's much nicer than I was, probably I should say than I am. She's helpful and thoughtful and thinks I'm someone to be served and admired. It isn't good for me."

Kel laughed.

"Stop it. Accept the fact that you are not perfect and just do the best you can."

"What do you mean I'm not perfect?" She made a face, mocking herself. "I just don't think I'm cut out to be a mentor. I'm not used to having to consider someone else all the time. Too selfish I suppose."

"Will you stop it." He was not laughing now. "As far as being a mentor is concerned you are no better and no worse than anyone else. All this introspection is not helpful. I might even dare to suggest it is self indulgent." He scowled at her with mock ferocity. "And if you keep it up I might have to take disciplinary action."

"Yes sir, sorry sir."

She sketched a little salute then found to her horror that she was crying. She turned her head away and got up to go and hide. Kel took hold of her.

"It's really getting to you, isn't it?"

She tried to run away then gave up and hid her face against his chest.

"I don't feel like myself at all," she said when she could speak unemotionally. "I go along pretending I'm grown up and sensible and sometimes it seems to work, sometimes I can even enjoy it, but other times I hate it. I didn't want to be a mentor, but Yarla and Jik and Fali all made me feel I'd be letting the Silberay down if I didn't accept an apprentice."

145

"And so you would have been," Kel said. "And letting yourself down too. You've never refused a challenge that I know of."

He held her away from him so he could see her face.

"Most of the Silberay would think that the other challenges you've accepted have been more difficult than this one. You didn't find it easy being Harbour Master either I seem to remember but you gave it your best effort and made a really worth while job of it. You can do the same with this."

He smiled at her.

"Don't try to be grown up and sensible, just be yourself and I think you'll find that you are grown up and sensible when you need to be, and Gelis will enjoy the times when you are not."

He pulled her into a hug.

"And now we will sing."

* * * *

Gelis followed the woman for perhaps half a mile. At first Loc kept ahead of them both, but when their subject turned into a side street he needed to retrace his steps and ended up some distance behind Gelis. The woman walked briskly without looking back. Gelis wondered whether she should try to get a bit closer, but it did not seem as if it would benefit her. The street, as far as she could see, held no surprise turnings and if the woman went into a house she thought she was close enough to be able to pick which one.

She had risked glancing back, just once, to check that Loc had seen her turn but then kept her eyes ahead, trying to keep her gaze casual and unfocused. The woman was, after all, Yareblis, and perhaps might sense her presence if she concentrated too hard on watching her. There was an intersection just visible ahead but before they reached it the woman crossed the road and went into one of the houses.

Gelis walked slowly past just glancing sideways to be sure she would recognise it again. It would not be difficult. The house was one of the few dwellings standing apart in its own grounds. It seemed to Gelis to have some of the same qualities as the Yareblis club, large, impersonal, overshadowing its neighbours with a sense of self importance and ostentatious grandeur.

She headed towards the distant intersection and waited around the corner for Loc to catch up. There was time to make a note of the street names and see if she could pinpoint her position on one of the sketch maps in her pocket before he reached her.

"That was worthwhile," he said, swinging into the side street where she waited. "I bet she doesn't live there alone."

They set off together along the footpath.

"I've found it on the map," Gelis said. "And there is a symbol. If we keep going this way, I think we will eventually reach somewhere on the bus route."

Loc nodded.

"Yes. I think we can consider it a day now."

They walked on together, quietly pleased with their day's work.

"It's nice to feel useful," Gelis commented.

Loc nodded.

"Especially when it is something like this, involved with our real work and not just cooking and washing up."

Gelis sighed.

"Marheh mostly insists we share those kinds of jobs. I'd really like to look after her more than she will let me."

Loc thought about his response.

"I have the impression that she has always been very independent," he said at last. "Just from comments Kel has made, but I'm guessing it will change as she gets older."

"It must be hard, getting older, losing some of the abilities you value," Gelis said. "But..."

"But?" Loc asked when it seemed she would not continue.

"Well, I... what I'm trying to say is, even if she can't do physical things, the disciplines will keep getting stronger won't they?"

Again Loc took time over his answer.

"As I understand it, the discipline of the soul will strengthen as long as it is practised until, in the end, we become all soul, but the mind can be broken."

"Not Marheh's," Gelis said firmly and increased her pace a little.

"Even Marheh's," Loc said hurrying to catch up with her. "If she meets a stronger mind, or has to confront more than one. It could happen. You saw how she was after her last encounter. But she is very strong and she has Kel's support."

Gelis remembered how she had seen Marheh, tired and dishevelled, sleeping and vulnerable, as well as experiencing her strength as she helped her to recognise a Yareblis illusion or supported her beginning song.

She sighed.

"I don't really understand about the discipline of the mind."

"How could you?" Loc said sympathetically. "Most of us take years to be able to communicate with our mentor and a lifetime to even approach the kind of thing Marheh does."

They had been thinking about their conversation rather than their walking but now they reached a crossroads and stopped to look about.

"Do we know where we are?" Loc said.

"The intersection of Garvey St and Mason Rd," Gelis said, reading from the street signs on the lamp post above them.

"Yes, but where is that?"

"Somewhere in Clanning," Gelis said flippantly.

Loc gave her a look and she fished in her pocket for the sketch maps. They poured over them but since they had not named many streets other than those with symbols it was difficult to make much sense of them.

"What do you think? Should we go back the way we came or keep walking and hope?" Gelis asked.

Loc looked again at their little maps and shrugged.

"What do you think?"

"Keep walking, but veer a bit south if we can because we came north of the town centre."

"As good a plan as any. No doubt if we get hopelessly lost we can find someone to ask."

* * * *

Marheh emerged from the song feeling more positive about herself and about life in general. Although the singing had not taken her adventuring or allowed her to spin her golden light it had been gently comforting, showing her she was not alone, giving her the perspective that she needed. Kel had been part of the music of course, but there had been many other singers and she had been just one of them, not important or special, but she understood that she would have been missed if she had not been there.

She drowsed on her bed for a little, allowing her thoughts to wander, wondering how Gelis and Loc were faring, thinking she should remind Kel to replace his control before they got under way again.

She said as much when he knocked and came in with sperit for her.

"Tomorrow will do," he said easily. "You're not thinking we will set off tonight are you?"

"I suppose not," she said. "But it means another whole day here if we don't."

"Perhaps we should wait and see how Gelis and Loc got on before we make any decisions. They will probably be tired."

"If we went to bed early and slept until two we could be there by five. There's no point in hanging about."

Kel searched her face but he could see that the song had renewed something in her. He nodded.

"If that's what you want."

"As long as Gelis and Loc are not too tired." She sat up and took her drink. "They ought to be getting back soon."

* * * *

By the time they had walked for fifteen minutes or so Gelis and Loc found themselves in quite a different environment. Here were no tall houses with front gardens. Instead the buildings were small and crammed together. Most seemed run down, some even looked as if they were barely standing. It was not a comfortable place to be and they quickened their steps almost involuntarily.

"Imagine if this was all you could afford," Gelis said. "It would be hard to be positive about anything."

"It would be hard not to feel envious of people with houses like that Yareblis woman has," Loc said.

Not far ahead of them they heard the sound of a door slamming and saw a man step onto the footpath. He turned and came towards them, hurrying as if on some urgent errand. Gelis stepped behind Loc and they moved to the edge of the footpath to allow him to pass. He was not looking at them and would have gone past without stopping but Gelis, startled to recognise him, spoke his name.

He stopped and glared at her.

"Karl, I'm so sorry, you've obviously lost your job like I have."

She had never seen him in anything but his clean, white, well-fitting uniform but now he seemed scruffy and down at heel.

"What are you talking about?"

He seized her arm. She tried to pull away.

"Here, let go of her."

Loc stepped forward.

"Why should I? She's just a kitchen hand." Karl's grip tightened. "Madam needs a kitchen hand."

"Karl, let go."

Loc made a grab for Karl who let go of Gelis and swung at him. His fist connected with the side of Loc's head. He staggered. Karl kicked. Loc's feet went from under him and he fell heavily, the loaded backpack unbalancing him.

"Loc!"

Gelis began to go to him. Karl grabbed her again, twisting her arm behind her back. She tried to break free, to kick him. He half pushed, half carried her back the way he had come.

* * * *

When Loc, stunned and disoriented, finally managed to gather himself, she was nowhere to be seen. He struggled to his feet and stood steadying himself against the nearest wall, trying to make sense of what had happened. She had recognised the man. Someone she had worked with at the club, but not Yareblis. Yareblis did not sully themselves with fisticuffs. Gelis wouldn't have left him if she could help it. Where would he have taken her? There had not been time for him to go far. He'd come from somewhere ahead. Could he pick which place? They all looked the same.

He began to stumble down the footpath, holding himself together with difficulty. Which one? All the front doors opened straight onto the pavement. Was it this one? The next one? He made his choice and hammered on the door, held his aching head for a moment or two then hammered again, but there was no response.

The attack had been so unexpected. He had never needed to involve himself in a physical fight before. Silberay fought with their minds if they fought at all. Mostly they tried to reason, to reconcile and conciliate. He looked up and down the scruffy little street half hoping that Gelis would appear from some odd corner. It was no good though, he would have to try to communicate with Kel. He had let everyone down and now their careful planning was useless, Marheh's sacrifice unnecessary and Gelis in danger.

He crossed the road and sat on the kerb. At least he could watch the houses and Gelis would see him if she was anywhere near. His head was aching and it was all he could do to put that outside him and try to focus, to build a picture of his mentor that would call to him and alert him to his need.

* * * *

On *Day Bringer* Marheh and Kel had begun preparations for the evening meal. Provisions were getting low and they had half expected Loc and Gelis to have returned with their bit of shopping by now, but since they had not what was still in the cupboard would have to suffice.

151

Marheh was beginning to be uneasy again but said nothing. She knew Kel was aware of her anxiety, perhaps even shared it. She was just passing him the tin opener when she saw him turn inward and recognised that he had been called. What had gone wrong? All she could do to help the communication was to contain her concern and open herself to listen. She touched him lightly and tried to make herself a kind of amplifier.

The contact did not last long.

"Loc?" Marheh asked when she knew Kel was back with her.

He nodded.

"I think he is hurt. Communication was difficult, but I saw a fight and a row of houses."

"Gelis?"

Kel shook his head.

"I don't think she was with him."

"She wouldn't have lift him if he was hurt, not if she could help it."

"No."

Marheh covered her face with both hands for a moment then looked up and reached across to turn off the gas under the saucepan.

"We'd best be away then, the sooner the better."

"*Day Bringer* or *Boat B*?" Kel asked.

Marheh looked surprised. She had not considered any possibility other than *Day Bringer*.

"It would make sense to use the Yareblis boat, wouldn't it?" she said slowly. "We'd be less likely to be noticed."

Kel nodded. He had hoped she would see it that way.

"If you get *Day Bringer* sorted out I'll go and check *Boat A*."

He gave her a brief hug and departed. She stood for a moment trying to collect herself enough to think calmly about what needed to be done. Gelis would not be served if she acted impulsively. One step at a time, first check the doors to the well deck and the windows in her cabin, next bank the fire and check the windows in the saloon and the galley, then check the stove, walk through the bathroom and the engine room, pause in Gelis' cabin to think of her and grab *Day Bringer*'s keys from their hook by the back door, lock the back doors and finally check the moorings were secure.

Kel was beside her for this last, knowing that she was hating abandoning *Day Bringer*. Together they walked to *Boat B* throbbing quietly in place. Marheh took up the mooring line and held it while Kel stepped into the cockpit and took the wheel. He gave her a nod and she put a foot on the gunnel, pushed gently with the other foot and they were away.

* * * *

Gelis struggled and fought as she was propelled down the road. Once inside the house Karl released her. She swung around to face him more angry than afraid.

"What do you think you're doing?"

He stood with his back against the door and stared at her without speaking.

"I suppose you didn't get paid either," she said. "I don't know why you think I can help you."

Still he did not move or speak. He'd not spoken much in the club kitchen either. She knew he thought it beneath him to converse with the kitchen hand. She had seen him seek Madam's approval, falling over himself to do her bidding and resenting any instruction to Gelis that was not communicated through him.

"Madam requires a kitchen hand," he said at last. "I am not a kitchen hand, I am a chef."

"I'm not a kitchen hand either," Gelis said. "I'm a...a...., I'm a just a student wanting a bit of pocket money to keep me going, which I did not get."

"Madam requires a kitchen hand," Karl said again.

"What has that got to do with me?"

Gelis glanced along the passageway where she found herself then back at Karl. He had possession of the front door and as far as she could tell there was no other exit.

"You'd better let me go out to my friend," she said, taking a tentative step towards him. "You must have hurt him."

Karl neither moved nor spoke.

"Where were you going anyway?" Gelis said after a short pause. "You looked as if you were in a hurry. Don't let me stop you."

"Madam requires a kitchen hand."

"Perhaps it is you she wants," Gelis said. "You would be much more useful than I would be."

"I am not a kitchen hand."

"Well neither am I." Gelis spoke as firmly as she could and drew herself up to look Karl in the eye. "You have no business keeping me here. If Madam wants you, you had better go to her."

She took a deep breath and stepped towards him again.

"Now move out of the way please."

For a moment she thought it had worked. He moved sideways as if to let her pass but as she reached him he gripped her arm and pulled her back from the door.

"For goodness sake Karl, don't be stupid!"

She tried to wrench herself free. He held on for a few moments then let her go so suddenly that she staggered backwards. She stood for a moment, breathing hard and trying to collect herself. He watched her without speaking.

"What is it you want?" she said at last.

"A kitchen hand for Madam. You."

We followed a Yareblis woman home
Then lost our way.
Never mind, we'll make it back
Sometime today.

Trouble struck. My mentor acted
Through my mind.
Placed a control on the enemy
His feet to bind.

We ran together, side by side
And caught the bus,
Happily going home again
The two of us.

Gelis

CHAPTER TWELVE

As *Boat B* moved into the channel, Marheh coiled the mooring line then stepped into the cockpit beside Kel.

"Do you need me for a bit?" she asked. "I might see whether I can find Gelis."

Kel nodded, his eyes on the water road, his mind busy with possibilities.

"Then we can exchange," she went on, knowing he would be concerned for Loc.

He nodded again.

"We might be best to go slowly until we can approach in darkness," he suggested.

"I'll see if I can find out more, find Gelis, before we decide to slow down," she said.

Boat B did not feel homelike nor conducive to abandoning herself to the discipline of the mind, but she had to try.

There was a kind of bench seat running against the side of the cockpit. It was not very comfortable despite its plastic covered cushion, but she would be near Kel and that seemed to her to be important. She tucked herself into the corner where it met the front of the cockpit and stretched her legs along the seat. At least she was rested now, her mind awake and ready to focus.

Closing her eyes she concentrated on building a picture of Gelis, making it as sharp and clear as she could without allowing herself to predict any expression. Expression must show itself without her willing it and, if it did, she would know she was getting close to her.

For sometime she held Gelis' image in the front of her mind, her curls, her brown eyes, her mouth with its slight upward curve, the tiny, barely noticeable scar above her left eyebrow, relic of a childhood mishap. Her mind ranged with the image, further and further, seeking the original, wanting to offer love and comfort.

At last she began to recognise a hint of life in her portrait. Her mind's ranging narrowed and narrowed again until the portrait and the living being became one.

She saw that Gelis was angry and anxious and recognised that her mind had not been threatened. So far so good. Now she needed to go very carefully. Gelis had experienced how it felt to have Marheh's mind walk beside her, but then she had not known what she was experiencing. Then there had been no danger that she would acknowledge Marheh's presence in a way that might alert an enemy. Now, if the Yareblis had her, Marheh's communication might make them aware that she was Silberay.

* * * *

Gelis stared at Karl.

"You have to be joking!" she said at last. "I didn't get paid for the work I did for her, why should I want to do more?"

"What you want is not important."

He stood, still blocking the door, and watched her disdainfully.

"It is to me."

He did not reply. Gelis stood opposite him, thinking furiously. What was the way out of this standoff? He obviously was not planning to hurt her, but he would stop her leaving. She was worried about Loc too. How badly was he hurt? Had he been able to communicate with Kel? Would he be able to help her if she managed to get outside? Was there anything she could do to help herself or to further the plans they had made together?

"Alright then," she said at last. "Why don't we go to Madam and I'll tell her myself that I don't want the job."

Karl studied her suspiciously.

"Go to Madam?"

"That's what I said. Isn't that what you want?"

She went towards him. He took her arm in a strong grip and turned to open the door. As he pulled her through Gelis glimpsed Loc sitting on the kerb opposite and knew he had seen her. She shook her head slightly. It would be best if he could follow not try to intervene.

Once he had pulled the door shut Karl began to hustle her along the footpath. They had gone only a few yards when Gelis began to recognise that she was not alone. The warmth she was feeling could only be Marheh and her heart leapt with thankfulness as her mind made her welcome.

Karl was still hustling her along, but now Marheh was in her mind and she was showing her where she was and what was happening. It seemed to her that Marheh was asking her consent for something. She did not know what it was but she gave it without reservation. She would trust Marheh with her life.

A few more steps then Karl stopped still. He continued to hold her arm but his grip could be broken. When Gelis had freed herself he remained in place. She turned to look at him but he did not move and she began to understand that he was controlled. Loc came up behind him a question on his face.

"I think Marheh did it," Gelis said.

"Marheh!" Loc looked about him.

"She's in my mind," Gelis said.

"Can you tell her what is happening?"

"I don't know. Perhaps if I make a picture she will understand but maybe we should move away from here first. Are you alright?"

He nodded.

"You look a bit wobbly. You'd better let me have the pack."

He made a token protest but was happy to relinquish it when she insisted.

"I'm not sure about the eggs," he said as she swung it onto her back.

"That's the least of our worries, come on."

She took a last look at Karl, still and expressionless, one hand holding the shape that had been her arm, one foot slightly ahead of the other as if he was about to step forward.

"I'm sorry Karl," she said quietly. "I don't think you'll be stopped for long."

Loc looked at her, but did not comment and together they stepped out along the street, continuing towards where they expected to find the bus route, or, at least, the road to the town centre.

* * * *

Operating *Boat B* did not take much of Kel's attention now that he was practised with the steering wheel. He was very aware of Marheh and understood that her mind was voyaging. Her closed eyes and quiet face gave him no clue to what she was finding and he was tempted to moor so that he could join her.

There had been no further communication from Loc and he was worried about him too. He eased back the throttle. Rushing into things was never a good idea. The Yareblis would be looking out for him, wanting to exult over his supposed capture of Marheh. If they arrived in Clanning too soon the need to continue their masquerade would inhibit their ability to help Loc and Gelis. He slowed still further until he barely had steerage. If Gelis had felt really threatened he thought it likely that Marheh would have heard her. Loc had shown him he had been in a fight, but that was not the Yareblis way. They would have used mind control, not physical force.

The next time he glanced towards Marheh he saw her beginning to stir. Her eyes opened.

"They're together and coming back," she said.

She looked pale and drained and Kel could see the effort she was making to act normally. She swung her feet off the seat and sat straighter.

"You could moor, I think, or we could even go back to *Day Bringer* if there is a place to turn."

"We've not gone very far, less than an hour's journey," Kel said. "I'll try to find Loc and suggest they come to us here. We can decide what to do when they arrive."

Marheh nodded.

"Best wait a little though, until they are away from whatever it was that caused the problem."

Kel was already busy mooring and did not answer, but he did not really need to. Marheh stood up to go to help but by the time she had got her limbs into working order he had finished and was back on board. She sat down again with a bit of a thump and sighed. Kel sat down beside her.

"Why don't we sing while we wait for them," he said.

The song was lifted with surprisingly little effort, as if a host of singers was awaiting their entry in order to feel the music complete. Melodies and counter melodies came and went with a pulsing rhythm that radiated further and further from the centre that was the bright gold of their music. Together they wove harmonies that stretched the reach of the light, pouring themselves out to dissolve the dark edges that threatened to enclose, to imprison, even perhaps extinguish the song that was their essence.

There was a limit to their reach and inevitably a time when their contribution to the music must end. They may have slept briefly afterwards but they woke feeling encouraged and supported. Kel sent his mind seeking Loc, who had been half expecting him. Their communication, though brief, was enough to guide the two apprentices as they approached the water road and it was not very long before Marheh and Kel saw them walking towards them along the tow path.

It was very clear to the two mentors that Gelis and Loc had had enough by the time they reached them. There was insufficient accommodation for them all on *Boat B* so returning to *Day Bringer* and *Boat A* was the only option. Kel stepped off to release the mooring while Marheh started the engine and took the wheel.

She found a spot where *Boat B* could squeeze around and soon they were on their way back. Gelis sat beside her with Loc while Kel stood ready to take over the wheel if Marheh wanted a break. Conversation was limited to brief queries as to well being. Sharing the real information the apprentices had gathered could wait until they were back with the other boats.

It did not take very long, even the need to find another turning place only added an extra ten minutes to the journey. Nevertheless it was beginning to get dark by the time *Boat B* was moored in place ahead of *Day Bringer* and all four were feeling hungry. *Day Bringer* had the most space so they gathered there to eat. Marheh and Kel insisted on waiting on Loc and Gelis and would not let them share their adventures until the meal was over. Once the table was cleared however they unfolded the map of Clanning and listened while Loc and Gelis told what they had learned.

"You've done a great job," Marheh said when it seemed they had finished. "I'm just sorry you had that trouble at the end."

"Loc is the one who suffered most," Gelis said, looking across the table at him.

"I'm alright," he said. "It's been worthwhile I think."

"Very much so," Marheh said. "When we get to Clanning it will be much more efficient to be able to go straight to the places you've identified."

"So when do we go?" Kel asked.

Marheh hesitated. She would like to get the next steps over with now that her mental energy was restored but she was conscious that Gelis and Loc needed to rest. She looked from one to the other.

"Would you be able to manage on six hours sleep?" she asked. "If we could set off about three in the morning we could be in Clanning before it wakes."

She was conscious that the control she had placed on Karl, though it had not lasted long, might have alerted the Yareblis to

Silberay presence. The sooner they could get closer to where she must act the better.

Loc and Gelis looked at each other.

"I'll be fine," Gelis said. "I'll set my alarm."

"Now that I've eaten I can be ready for anything," Loc said.

"Then that is what we'll do," Marheh said. "You two get off to bed. Kel and I will do the dishes."

Once their apprentices had disappeared Marheh and Kel looked at each other.

"I'm sorry if I've taken over," Marheh murmured as Kel put his arms around her.

He laughed and held her close for a few minutes.

"We'd better get those dishes out of the way and get some sleep ourselves," he said at length.

"You'd better replace your control too, just in case," Marheh said.

Three o'clock came quickly, before Marheh was ready for it really, but it was no good putting off the necessary action any longer and at least this way she had the chance to take the initiative. She dressed quickly, choosing a warm undershirt and tunic against the chill of the morning. The sky was bright with stars and she took a moment to gaze and marvel, refreshing her spirit with its beauty.

Gelis was up and dressing too, she knew, feeling *Day Bringer* move in the water. They would not waste time with breakfast but sperit would be warming. She went through to put the kettle on and found that Gelis had had the same idea and was already spooning the mixture of spices and dried berries into their mugs while the kettle was warming on the stove.

"What a treasure," Marheh teased. "And sensible too, no light on to spoil our night vision."

Gelis turned to grin at her.

"Will the others come here for sperit?"

"I should think so. Shall I take a look?"

161

The kettle began to whistle loudly and *Day Bringer* rocked as Kel and then Loc boarded. A moment later they were all together, looking at each other over their steaming mugs. Teeth and eyes showed bright in their shadowed faces and tension kept them standing, unable to relax. Marheh was aware that Gelis and Loc were excited at the adventure ahead and was able to be glad that they did not know enough to share her fears. Kel understood though and she felt his sympathy warm and calm her.

"Ready?"

Marheh rinsed and dried her mug and replaced it on its hook.

"Ready."

Loc and Gelis rinsed their cups and headed off to *Boat B*.

"Are you ready?" Kel asked, dealing with his mug.

"As I'll ever be," Marheh said lightly.

They went out to the back deck together.

"No one will notice that you are not bound," Kel said as she went to the tiller.

"No, I suppose not. With any luck no one will see us at all until we get there."

She stepped off to release *Day Bringer*'s mooring while Kel continued to *Boat A*. Loc started the engine on *Boat B* then she heard *Boat A*'s engine give a little cough and purr into life. It seemed wrong not to be starting *Day Bringer*'s engine too, but that was the part she was playing.

Very slowly the cavalcade set off. Marheh leaned against the railing around the back deck and let her mind drift. For the moment, she had nothing to do except watch the night slowly pass. Nearer to Clanning she might rehearse the action she must take but too much introspection was not helpful. They had discussed how they would proceed. Circumstances might alter their planning but just now she knew how she would begin and anxious re-examination would only sap her mental strength.

The night sky washed the rather dull landscape with a silvery light that transformed it into a scene of beauty and mystery. There were dark shadowed shapes that hugged the land and then revealed themselves as low trees and shrubs, there were pale stretches of grassy pasture and the occasional lane, almost white against the hedges that ran beside and the dark bulk of the bridge that carried it over the water road. Nothing moved except the three boats.

Marheh began gently exercising her mind, preparing for the focussed effort she would need later by setting herself to listen to the landscape. There was work she could do here, but not yet. First she must deal with the Yareblis.

An hour or more went past before the roof tops of Clanning showed themselves against the sky and, not long after, the water road began to be confined between fences and the walls of buildings. Marheh's attention heightened. Anticipation and a hint of the fear she kept firmly suppressed were used to sharpen her focus. Would there be Yareblis waiting for them? Would Kel need to activate his control, and if he did what would it mean for her, for them all? It was no good worrying. She was rested and ready. She could probably deal with two or three together. Kel was there to support her. She would not think about the possibility of failure.

Very quickly, too quickly it seemed, they approached the mooring. Although Marheh had glimpsed a pedestrian or two as the streets of Clanning were carried across the water road, she had no sense that they were observed. Gelis and Loc had seen boats at the mooring though. There may well be Yareblis about there. Kel would need to show he had her controlled.

It would be better if she did not have to act against them while they were in sight of the water road. However swiftly and subtly she worked, if the water road vanished in front of them they would know what she had done.

They were aware from Gelis and Loc's report that there would not be room for them to moor in line as they were. The Yareblis boats were shorter, but even so, three of them would use almost the whole length of the dock.

Loc drew them slowly under the canopy. He saw that there was room for either *Boat B* or *Boat A* against the dock but not for both, and definitely not for *Day Bringer*. Marheh would have no choice. She would have to cross a Yareblis boat to get to the dock. He began to edge *Boat B* past the first of the Yareblis boats. There was not much room and he was concentrating hard. Gelis stood ready to fend off if necessary.

Behind on *Day Bringer* Marheh saw the welcoming committee emerge and her heart sank. She would need to go on playing the prisoner. Two men stepped out of one of the Yareblis boats and stood on the dock watching. Kel saw them too and prepared himself to act. He recognised one of the men from the earlier encounter at the bridge and shouted a demand that he take the line he held ready to throw him.

Marheh did not move. She would wait now for Kel's control, but she could use these moments to assess, approaching the Yareblis mind with a feather touch. She reached the one who was distracted by his work for Kel and understood that he would not pose much of a threat but as she turned her attention to the other she realised that she knew him and drew back.

It was the Club Treasurer. He would know at once that she was not controlled if she touched his mind. She had only met him once when he called on her family at the pottery, but he had recognised her then and issued a challenge. He would have come to gloat over her supposed captivity and for the moment she would have to allow it, but only for the moment.

She remained still, facing ahead. Getting the three boats sorted would take a little time. Kel would have to direct all her movements now. At least Loc and Gelis were beneath the notice of the Club Treasurer. He would be concerned only with Kel, who had demonstrated his strength and status by capturing her. The fact that Kel was unknown to him would make him curious and a bit wary but the story they had planned should account for it. As far as she knew the Yareblis did not work cooperatively, nor did they gather in community as the Silberay did. They used power even over each other and their place in the hierarchy depended on how strong they were. There was no reason why the Club Treasurer should know Kel and every reason why he would not want to lose face by testing himself against him.

She heard the rumble of Kel's voice as he spoke to the two Yareblis. He was good at dissembling. His arrogant tones and clipped sentences did not sound at all like him. Then she found herself moving. This was the part that he hated doing. She knew he found it difficult to make her act in any way that might humiliate her. She didn't like it herself, but it was what the Club Treasurer would want to see and if Kel couldn't bring himself to be unkind enough she would have to act for him.

He was in control for the moment though, making her step away from the tiller, across *Day Bringer*'s deck and onto the Yareblis boat, then across the Yareblis boat to the dock. As he had done before, he made her kneel, not to the Club Treasurer but to him, emphasising his power over her. The Club Treasurer stepped closer, lifted her plait and pulled it so that her head jerked back.

"There will be time for that later," Kel said coldly.

Marheh sent him a little warmth.

"I have it controlled. Now I claim the reward."

Marheh bent lower until her forehead touched the ground.

"Where do I take it?"

"Come with me," the Club Treasurer said.

The pleasure and anticipation in his voice sickened her. She would not have been surprised if he had kicked her from behind, but Kel, perhaps anticipating some such action , was strolling around her in lordly fashion so that he was unable to get close to her. Then he had her stand again.

"I will just instruct my assistants," Kel said, walking across the dock to where he could see Loc and Gelis waiting on *Boat B*, trying not to look as anxious as they felt.

"You will remain here until sent for," he ordered them.

His voice was still cold and arrogant but before turning away he winked at them. Loc muttered something that might have been 'yes sir'. Gelis remained silent. He had not left Marheh for more than a couple of minutes, but when he turned back he saw that the Club Treasurer was standing in front of her staring into her eyes and telling her how the Yareblis would take their revenge. He wanted to punch the man's gloating face but managed to control his anger.

"This way I assume," he said moving Marheh towards the door.

"Aren't you going to bind it?" the other Yareblis asked.

Kel thought he sounded scared.

"What for? I have it controlled."

The Club Treasurer jerked his head at the exit and the other Yareblis hurried to open it. Marheh walked through. Kel and the Club Treasurer followed. The other Yareblis waited until they were together on the pavement before shutting the door and going to join them.

Marheh stood waiting for Kel to control her and remembering Clanning as it had been when first she visited it. She had been with Nemle then, not wearing her uniform, not showing herself as Silberay, but wearing an old blue skirt and a long grey cardigan, just an ordinary young woman with her grandmother.

This part of town had not changed much. She could remember the route to the town hall. She and Nemle had gone there to confront the Yareblis who had managed to gain too much power over the people of Clanning. Would it be the town hall this time, she wondered, setting off up the hill under Kel's control.

Doing only what Kel told her to do left her mind free to consider their situation. She knew she could disable the other Yareblis without him even being aware but the Club Treasurer was a different matter. Part of the problem was disposal of the water dimension once she had excised it. It was painful to contain within her own mind and the stronger the enemy the more uncomfortable it would be. Kel had devised a technique whereby he created in his mind a small box where several of the ugly distortions that she took could be stored without too much discomfort, but controlling her, even though she was so acquiescent, would be using some of his mental energy. The only permanent means of disposal was fire and that was not always as accessible as it had been in the past when every house had a working fire place and every pub an open fire for customers to enjoy.

Kel's control was still prompting her every action and in consequence she was not paying a great deal of attention to her steps. It was so early that there were very few people about. The shops were still closed and the only vehicle she had seen was a garbage truck. She walked on, a little ahead of the men, until Kel stopped her at an intersection. He turned her towards him and had her bow deferentially before directing her down the side street.

She and Kel had studied the map carefully after Loc and Gelis had reported their findings and she had done her best to remember the significant landmarks. Now she guessed they were moving towards the area where they had discovered Yareblis lived. Would it be Westall St or the home of the Yareblis woman, or perhaps the person Gelis had called the Odd Messenger. She could only continue walking and hold herself ready when the chance came to act.

*****

Back at the mooring, Loc and Gelis were finding the waiting difficult.

"But he winked at us, I saw him," Gelis argued. "Surely he didn't mean for us to stay here."

"The wink was just to show us he was pretending to be harsh. He does expect us to stay with the boats unless he sends for us."

"How can he send for us?"

"He can communicate with me even if I can't respond very well and it's easier for him if he knows where I am."

"We can't do anything to help if we're stuck here."

"But we won't get in the way either."

Gelis was nearly in tears.

"I hate what Marheh is doing. It's too real. You saw how he treated her."

"She and Kel have worked together for years. They know what they're doing. We can help them best by staying here."

Loc looked sympathetically at Gelis.

"We can wait on *Day Bringer* if you like, empty the loo and fill the water tank if you want to do something useful. It won't matter, even if someone sees us there we can pretend to be researching the Silberay."

Gelis nodded.

"I'd like that, if you're sure it won't matter."

*****

Like Marheh, Kel was wondering just where they were heading. He was not comfortable with what they were doing. He might be controlling Marheh's steps, but the whole plan was hers and he knew her well enough to expect surprises. She had hoped to arrive unnoticed so she could enter and disable sleeping minds. It was why they had agreed that Loc and Gelis should explore in Clanning. Everything would be much more difficult now. Marheh would perhaps be mocked and humiliated and he would have to pretend to accept, even enjoy that, if he was to continue the charade.

For the moment though, he needed to dismiss every concern of his and focus entirely on directing Marheh's steps, listening for any communication from her mind and maintaining his character as Yareblis. He was grateful that he did not need to be affable. It meant that he did not need to converse or do more than grunt in response to most remarks.

He was not really surprised when he saw they were entering Westall Road. Gelis had reported that she had been directed there when she demanded payment. Marheh had managed to let him know that their guide was the Club Treasurer. It made sense.

What did surprise him was the sudden realisation that Marheh was expecting him to take something from her.

*****

Walking, thinking, planning, Marheh tried not to dwell on the probability that she would have to allow herself to be humiliated, but to focus on the actions that would ultimately mean victory. The weaker of the two accompanying Yareblis offered little challenge. When she realised they were in Westall Road it seemed sensible to act and hope that Kel could contain what she took. Who knew what they might encounter once they went inside?

168

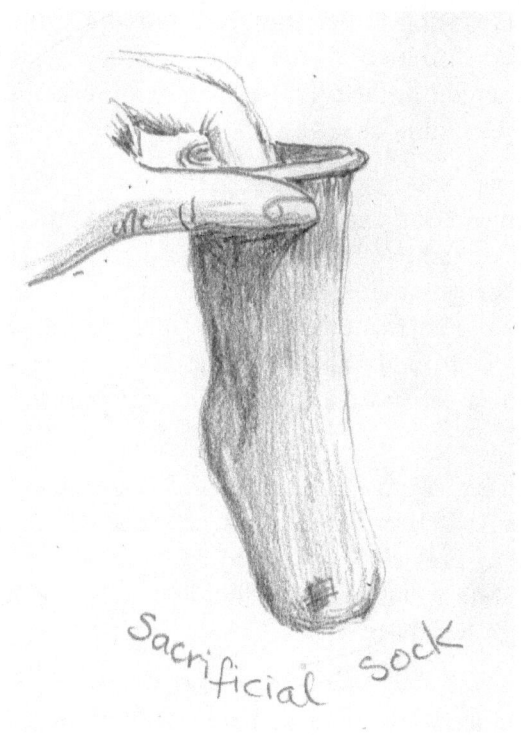

Sacrificial sock

CHAPTER THIRTEEN

Number 11 Westall Road was a tall, narrow house set in a row of tall, narrow houses. A fence of iron pickets enclosed a small, very neat, rather sterile, front garden. A short concrete path led from the front gate to the two steps that gave access to a little porch and the front door. It did not appear much different from its neighbours except perhaps for the rigid restraint imposed on the little plants in the borders.

Marheh found herself stopped a few steps past the entrance. Kel was careful not to reveal that he had guessed their destination. The Club Treasurer went ahead then to open the gate. As she was directed in and past him the gloating satisfaction in his gaze caused Marheh a moment of panic. What was she doing here? It was her choice to pursue the remaining Yareblis. No one would have blamed her if she had stopped with the rescue at Deerford. It was not just herself she was risking either, but Kel and the future of their two apprentices. She stumbled a little mounting the steps but recovered herself and waited, outwardly passive, while the Club Treasurer inserted his key and unlocked the door.

A long hallway was the first thing she saw. It was quite dimly lit but she could make out a staircase at the furthest end. About half way along a splash of light fell on the dark red runner that covered the hall floor and she saw that it came from an open door. She heard the sound of voices. The front door closed behind her. She was alone, trapped, isolated in a bubble of emptiness. Then Kel's warmth touched her for a second as he directed her steps towards the door and the voices.

It was not a big room she entered and it seemed crowded, full of avid anticipation. It was too late to run, too late for caution and commonsense to prevail. She wanted to whimper. What had she let herself in for? She fought to keep hold of the passion and purpose that had brought her there.

As she steadied she understood that the room held only eight people beside herself and Kel and one of them she had dealt with already. Perhaps things would not be as bad as she had feared, especially since she now noticed that the room was warmed by a small fire.

Kel too had noticed the fire and immediately made his way towards it, leaving Marheh standing in the centre of the room. He held his hands out to the warmth then rubbed them together, before turning back to Marheh.

"Quite a welcoming committee," he said to the Club Treasurer who had moved to stand beside him. "Obviously you recognise the importance of my prisoner."

He looked around the room and wondered whether Gelis would recognise any of its occupants. He thought perhaps the big woman in white might be the one she called Madam, she who had been the chef at the club. The other woman he recognised as the woman who had met them at the bridge. The two sat in armchairs in opposite corners of the room. The other two men from the bridge were there also. One stood by the curtained window while the other sat. Also sitting were two other men, one of whom occupied the largest and most opulent armchair in the room.

For a brief moment he allowed his mind to touch Marheh's.

"I'm ready," she sent, encouraging him to act.

"You wish me to demonstrate my control over it," he announced to the room at large.

The anticipation in the room heightened.

He had Marheh turn on the spot then kneel and rise again. This was the balancing act. While he controlled her, her mind was free to act. A moment later he knew she had. Another twisted water dimension from a Yareblis mind was passed to him. He added it to the one he already held, wondering which of the Yareblis she had disabled.

"Beginner's tricks."

The words came from the man in the big chair.

Kel raised his eyebrows.

"And you are?" he asked.

"Have it strip," the man demanded, leaving Kel's question unanswered.

Two down, six to go, Kel thought, wondering how long he could delay.

In the centre of the room Marheh bent to unlace her boots and pull them off. Kel would need to be rid of the two he held before she attempted to excise another. She took off one sock and went to him, offering the sock with a low bow. She sent him a picture of the sock burning. He took it from her and held it up.

"It will not need this again," he said and made a great production of putting it on the fire behind him. With it went the two water dimensions he held.

So far Marheh knew she had not been detected entering another mind, but it was becoming more and more difficult. The Yareblis who remained were strong and well defended. The small distraction of the burning sock had given her an opportunity that she had used and now she held another water dimension. Passing it to Kel was a possibility, but it might be more convincing if she sacrificed her other sock herself. She knew how much Kel was hating what he was doing, but if he did not keep doing it her mind would not be free to act. He picked up her thought and almost immediately she began to move towards the fire.

The sock and the water dimension were burning satisfactorily but it had not been enough of a distraction. She sent her mind ranging, looking for an opening. Dimly she understood that Kel was making her take off her tunic but it was not until her shirt had come off as well that another opportunity presented itself.

Perhaps she had been a little clumsy since Kel heard a kind of grunt from the woman who was not Madam, but there was no accusation. The woman was delving into the handbag at her feet. She pulled out a small gold coloured tube, removed part of it and plunged at Marheh. Kel's sudden fear might have given him away but all eyes had been on the woman who had opened her lipstick and was marking Marheh's back.

HA! HA! In large scarlet letters appeared on the skin above her bra, but the action had given her another opportunity.

Three left. How much more could she manage? How much more could she bear? Kel took what she gave him and turned to the fire. No one was interested in him now.

Bear or bare? The question came to him from Marheh's mind along with the image of a wry grin.

One of the men had taken the lipstick and another produced a ballpoint pen. Once more she acted, taking advantage of what seemed to Kel to be a kind of feeding frenzy as the group swarmed around her. The man with the lipstick gave her a clown's big red smile. The man with the ballpoint found a place on her upper arm to write. Other men produced pens and found skin to mark. Kel ached to be able to help her, to stop them, but he held himself back, knowing his best help was to take and burn that for which she was sacrificing herself. Two left. Even if she succeeded with them all they would be vengeful once they realised what she had done. He would need to have strength enough to get her away.

Marheh was only dimly aware of what was happening to her

physical self. Her mind was stretched, working with all its power. The two Yareblis she had yet to disable had recognised her attempts and now she was herself under attack. It was too much after all she had already done. All she could think of was Kel. They must not discover him. Let them take her, break her, if only she could keep them from suspecting his part in the masquerade.

His control was still within her. That was no masquerade, but she could not take refuge in him, not here among them. Suddenly the anxious face of her apprentice came into her mind. Gelis was thinking of her, wanting to help her. Could she take refuge there just for a few moments? In desperation she jumped as she had before and found herself held.

* * * *

Gelis and Loc had spent the waiting time on *Day Bringer* doing their best to practise their song. Worry had prevented them from entering for some time and neither felt as if they had succeeded in adding any melody, even the simplest baby tune, but trust in the teaching of their mentors kept them trying. Gelis kept seeing Marheh as she had been, kneeling to Kel, walking steadily, with set face, away from them. She longed to be of service to her, to give her what she could of her strength. Then, in an instant, her offering as accepted.

As before there was a moment of pain before she held something impossibly beautiful, fragile and paradoxically strong. She enfolded it with gentle care pouring out all the feelings of admiration and love she had for her mentor, wanting nothing more than to serve her. A few precious minutes and she was gone again, leaving a hint of warmth and gratitude.

* * * *

Kel thought his control was all that was keeping Marheh standing. She had given him another water dimension to destroy and now, he knew, she was fighting for her mind against her last opponent. It was so difficult to hold back, to trust that her strength would be sufficient, but if he joined her fight now he would have nothing left with which to protect her from these enemies once her task was accomplished. Losing their power to control would not stop them from wanting to be revenged, from taking revenge, unless he could control them for long enough to take her away back to the water road.

* * * *

Marheh was dissolving, disintegrating agonisingly by slow stages. Her hands had gone now, finger by finger, thumbs, palms. Her feet had begun to fragment.

"No crying," Nemle was telling her. "No crying."

"No crying," she was trying to repeat, but the tears kept coming.

"Big girls don't cry," her mother was saying. "No crying."

"No crying."

Mama and Nemle were gone now. Why were they here talking to her? Was she gone too? Why did they tell her not to cry when she was hurting so much?

"Hold on sweetheart, papa loves you."

How could she hold on with no hands?

"Hold on daughter, mama loves you."

"I'm holding."

"Hold on daughter of my heart, Nemle loves you."

"Hold on."

A ghostly impression of her hands twitched at the ends of her arms.

"Hold on."

"Hold on."

Gradually her vision cleared. Her hands might yet be whole enough to wield the scalpel and complete her task.

"Hold on niece, Jik loves you."

A surge of power pulsed through her and sharpened her focus. She saw the opening she needed and acted.

There was a moment of contact with Kel before she fell into the soul song.

* * * *

174

"We have to go," Gelis said. "They need us. We have to."

Loc was hard to persuade.

"I know. We have to."

"I haven't heard from Kel."

"I don't care. I know we have to go. I'll go without you if you won't come."

She pushed past him and up to the back deck.

"Alright, I'm coming."

Together they crossed the Yareblis *Boat A*nd stepped onto the dock.

"Hurry!"

* * * *

Kel only needed a moment or two at the fire but when he turned back to Marheh she was on the floor. He hurled a couple of controls at the two men closest to her then dived to her side as they froze in place. Now they were no longer Yareblis, controlling them was unopposed, but eight controls would test him.

It also revealed what Marheh had done. He acted quickly to forestall attempts at reprisal until there were still figures in armchairs and standing as well as lunging towards Marheh.

She lay sprawled, face down on the patterned square of carpet. The red slashes stood out starkly against her white skin and shocked him until he recognised they were lipstick. Her clothes had been pulled about by Yareblis wanting to write on her skin. Blue and black writing, scrawled names and taunts disfigured her.

Kel dashed aside his tears. He would not be able to control so many for long. The most important thing was to get her away. Gently he lifted her, held her against him to adjust her clothing, put her limp arms into the sleeves of her shirt, pull her tunic over her head and squeeze her bare feet into the boots abandoned beside her. He knelt then, tried to take her in his arms, but ended by putting her over his shoulder in a fireman's lift before staggering to his feet. Even this would not be possible for long but he could at least get her out of the house. Once outside he would carry her for as long as he could and

175

then hope to find a place to hide.

The front door was open when he reached it, an unexpected aid that he had no time to consider. The gate too was pulled back. Marheh still lay limp, a dead weight over his shoulder and he was desperately worried about her. Going on was the only option however, back the way they had come, as close to *Day Bringer* as he could manage. He had been able to carry her easily once, but now he was old. They both were really. Marheh would never be old. He had never felt like an old man. He did now though. Marheh had been his to love and care for, to complement, since forever, since they were both young. He would not fail her now.

The very first time they met she had been hurt and he had carried her in his arms. That was fifty years ago. She had been stubborn and outspoken, quick to take offence but equally quick to apologise. He had been awed by her talent. Even as an apprentice her ability at the discipline of the mind had been outstanding. It had not taken long for awe to be replaced by affection and then love. At twenty she had been young for her age and both his mentor and hers had helped him to value his own qualities of steadiness and strength and shown him how these could complement Marheh's gift.

There was a corner at the end of Westall Rd. He turned, thankful to be out of sight of the house. At least the way was down hill. He had rescued her on more than one occasion but never before had he had to witness the cost of her actions as they happened. Could he have saved her any other way? Did he have to allow them to abuse her?

Another corner. Every corner helped to reduce the possibility of pursuit, but he was not sure how much longer he could continue to carry her. The streets were beginning to wake. It was still quite early but there had been a boy on a bicycle delivering newspapers and a couple of vans. One had slowed as it passed almost as if the driver thought to offer assistance, but it had been travelling in the opposite direction and sped off again.

He turned another corner. Could he, perhaps, be half way to the mooring now? In the distance, coming towards him, were two figures. They were approaching quickly and a moment later he recognised his apprentice and Marheh's. They couldn't have come at a better time. A few minutes more and they met. Gently Kel lowered Marheh into Loc's arms. Gelis gasped at the sight of her face with its red clown smile.

"Is she…?"

Kel shook his head and urged them onward.

"We need to get to *Day Bringer* before my controls weaken."

Loc was striding out in front of Gelis and Kel.

"They could ambush us at the entrance to the mooring."

He was moving more easily now without Marheh's weight.

"Once we are in the water dimension we will be safe.'

"Should I run ahead?" Gelis asked. "I could check whether the mooring is being watched."

"They could get there ahead of us easily in a car," Loc said, pausing to adjust Marheh's weight.

She opened her eyes. He saw a moment of panic.

"It's Loc," he said, reassuring her.

Her eyes moved, seeking, until Kel moved into her field of vision then they closed again.

"Would it hurt Marheh to get wet?" Gelis asked, a bit tentatively.

Kel and Loc looked at her.

"I was just thinking," she said. "Maybe we could wade in from the pond. They wouldn't expect that."

Loc felt Marheh stir in his arms. Her eyes opened again and she mumbled something. Kel stood beside her.

"I think that's agreement," he said. "She'll be able to walk herself now, if we support her."

Carefully they set her down.

"Her mind is beginning to recover." Kel tried to explain to the two apprentices. "She has to remember how to walk and talk."

She stood between Kel and Loc. They were about to step out again when Gelis suddenly knelt to tie the trailing boot laces that Kel had ignored in his haste to get them away. Kel smiled at her as she stood again.

"Will you lead the way?"

It took them about fifteen minutes to reach the pond and by that time Marheh was almost in control of her limbs. Speech and movement together required more concentration so she had not attempted to talk as they went but once they stood together by the pond she managed a smile.

"Ready to take the plunge?" Kel asked.

They were close to the place where the water road entered. First Gelis and then Loc and Kel with Marheh between them, stepped off the neat surround and into the water. A morning jogger gave a shout and a man reading the newspaper on a park bench looked up in surprise. Gelis made for the water road. The shallow edge quickly stepped down until she was waist deep and swimming. The two men, both fairly tall, held Marheh between them and followed. Gelis, looking back to check their progress, saw the moment when they disappeared to the two startled spectators.

It was a bit further to the mooring than Marheh remembered. Last time she had been there the distance had seemed like nothing because she had been on *Day Bringer*. Now, although her mind was beginning to recover, she needed the help and support of the two men. They were tall enough to make wading relatively easy and she bobbed between them her feet off the bottom half the time. She could see Gelis ahead, swimming easily, turning back occasionally to check their progress.

There were buildings on either side of them, blank, windowless walls rising above them. It made the water road seem unfriendly. Marheh closed her eyes and concentrated on the kindly grip of Kel and Loc. Kindness mattered. Kindness was helping her heal and keeping her safe. Kindness and love were offering her mind a way back from the pain and isolation that were the price she paid for her actions against the Yareblis.

As they passed beneath it, the shadow of the roof over the mooring prompted her to open her eyes again. Gelis had already reached *Day Bringer* and was pulling herself up onto the back deck.

Water poured off her. She saw her stand and turn back to watch as they came closer. Then they were beside *Day Bringer* and heading for the back deck. Kel and Loc boosted her up. Gelis helped her move out of the way so that the two men had room to climb on board. She closed her eyes again.

"No you don't," she heard Kel say.

Her eyes remained closed. He couldn't possibly be expecting her to act now.

"Best if we don't trail water through *Day Bringer*," Kel said. "I'll look after Marheh. You two see what you can do about drying off."

She was not going to open her eyes, not yet. Kel might expect her to act. She felt the movement as Loc walked along the gunnel towards *Boat B* and heard the sound of Gelis' wet jeans and t-shirt landing on the deck. When she knew Gelis had gone below she opened her eyes. Kel was beside her.

"Come on you, up you get."

She closed her eyes again.

"No you don't."

His arms were underneath her, hoisting her to her feet.

"Mean," she muttered.

Then he was holding her, murmuring her name, his arms tight around her.

Dry clothes were a problem. Gelis was the only one of the four who had anything like a wardrobe. Loc and Kel had left theirs on *Storm Cloud* and Marheh's had already been reduced by her loss at the Clanning service area.

Fifteen minutes later Gelis and Loc were in the galley considering the possibilities for a late breakfast. Gelis was wearing her blue dress, Loc, his pyjamas. Kel and Marheh were in the bathroom. Kel too was wearing pyjamas. Marheh was wearing nothing at all. She sat on the edge of *Day Bringer*'s little hip bath with her back to Kel. He picked up her plait and moved it out of the way then kissed the nape of her neck and ran one finger gently along her spine. She turned her head to smile at him over her shoulder.

She had already attacked the clown smile they had given her and her face was clean and rather scrubbed looking. The graffiti on her back stood out sharply against her pale skin. Kel dipped a washer into warm soapy water and began to clean it off.

For a while he worked in silence. The marks were stubborn and he didn't want to hurt her. She rested in his care at first then her mind returned to remembering her last battle. There was something she needed to understand.

A few minutes later Kel saw her raise her hand and brush something from her face.

"Am I hurting you?"

She shook her head.

"What is it?"

She turned her head towards him and he saw her face was wet with tears.

"It's Jik," she said.

"Jik?"

He didn't understand. How could he, but she remembered the surge of power that had given her the strength she needed, remembered too the way those souls who had loved her in life had been there for her.

"I think he gave me the last of his life," she said. "Gave me the strength of his love... and... saved me."

Kel put down the washer and reached for Marheh's towel.

"He loved you," he said, wrapping it around her and lifting her so he could hold her.

She nodded and rested her head against his chest. A minute or two later she drew in a deep breath and moved back from him.

"I'd better get dressed," she said.

Purloined Provisions

CHAPTER FOURTEEN

Breakfast felt like an indulgence. Gelis and Loc had made pancakes and there was hot chocolate liberated from a supply they had discovered on *Boat B*. Loc and Kel were still in their pyjamas perforce, but Marheh had chosen to put on her best trousers rather than spend the day in her dressing gown.

"Loc and I have had an idea," Gelis said when the pancakes had disappeared. "We've thought about how to leave here without going into the pond where they can see us."

"Oh," said Marheh.

"Have you?" said Kel.

Gelis glanced at Loc then continued to speak.

"We saw that the other Yareblis boats, the three that were here when we arrived, are facing away from Clanning. We thought we could use two of them to pull *Day Bringer* out to the last turning place we passed."

She paused and looked at Loc again.

"And we would really like to do it ourselves," she finished in a rush.

"I see," Marheh said after a moment's pause. "Mutiny below decks is it?"

Gelis grinned.

"That's right, and you'd better do as you're told or we might make you walk the plank."

"Not in my best trousers, thank you," Marheh said.

She turned to Kel.

"What do you think, shall we indulge them?"

"Why not?"

"It's a good idea," Marheh said. "Much better than waiting until dark to turn *Day Bringer*, which is all my poor brain could come up with."

"I don't think the pond would take *Day Bringer*'s length now," Loc said. "It's very shallow at the edges."

"Which I wouldn't have realised in the dark."

Marheh gave a grin.

"Getting stuck would not be good for my image."

They laughed.

"We'll tidy up here and get started then," Loc said. "Is it okay if we take any food left on the Yareblis boats? *Day Bringer*'s stocks are a bit low."

Marheh and Kel looked at each other.

"They won't be able to get it, will they?" Loc went on. "It would just be wasted."

"I suppose so," Marheh said slowly. "Part of me would like to pay for it, but they wouldn't get the money either."

"Bring it on board," Kel said. "We'll see what there is and send a cheque. We know the address."

There was not very much, a couple of tins of tomatoes, some of fish and some of beans, hot chocolate powder, powdered milk and two bottles of wine. Kel made a rough estimate of the cost as Gelis put things away with *Day Bringer*'s stores.

"Are we running away?" Marheh asked Kel when Gelis and Loc had gone outside to begin the manoeuvre they had planned.

"No, I don't think so. We neither of us have fully recovered and even if we had I'm not sure what more we could do here just now."

"There will have been people controlled. Now the controls are broken, some, at least, might be confused about how to go back to the life they had before."

Kel nodded.

"But I don't think we would be any help even if we could find them. There must have been at least one who left Westall Road. That will be why the front door and the gate were open when I wanted to leave with you. It was a great help."

They were sitting opposite each other at *Day Bringer*'s little table. Kel reached across and took one of Marheh's hands.

"Watching them abuse you was perhaps the hardest thing I've ever had to do."

Marheh put her hand over his.

"It wasn't much fun being abused, but it worked. That's the important thing."

Outside they could hear the sound of *Boat B*'s engine starting up and then there was a little jerk as *Day Bringer* moved forward. Marheh raised her eyebrows.

"Do you think they know what they are doing?"

"I'm sure they do," Kel said firmly.

"Why are we going this way then?"

"Relax."

Gelis' legs went past the galley window walking along the gunnel.

"I can't watch."

Marheh put her head down on her outstretched arms.

"Don't be silly."

She lifted her chin to glare at him.

"Me! Silly!"

"Yes you."

She sighed.

"Perhaps I should just retire now and go and live at the Harbour."

The sound of another engine coughing into life reached them.

"I don't think there is any need for you to retire," Kel said, laughing at her. "But if you're going to be silly I might have to put you to bed."

Day Bringer stopped her forward movement and a moment later began to move backwards very slowly. They heard Gelis call to Loc and then his reply although they could not make out the words.

"Bed would be lovely, but not while all this is going on."

There was a sudden jerk as *Day Bringer* was pulled up short. The engine in front of *Day Bringer* died. Marheh went to get up but Kel held her where she was.

"You have to let them do it."

"But…"

"But nothing. Trust them."

Another engine started and then they heard Loc shout.

"Take her away."

Day Bringer slid slowly backwards past *Boat A*, moored by the dock, and out from the canopy into the light of what promised to be a lovely day. Marheh watched as they went under the bridge, watched as houses slid into view then sighed.

"Please sir, may I go and look now?"

Kel laughed at her again.

"I don't see why not. They seem to have everything under control. You can look and admire."

She made a face.

"And you have me under control so I won't spoil it for them."

Kel did a double take and she laughed this time.

"No, not literally. I could go out and insist on doing everything myself. I won't though, promise."

They got up from the table and made their way out to the back deck. One of the Yareblis boats was ahead of them, fastened to *Day Bringer* on a short line. They could see Gelis in the cockpit. She was obviously concentrating hard on her steering and did not look back although Marheh thought she was aware of their arrival.

The water road out of Clanning was very narrow, only one boat width in lots of places. It made towing a challenge. It was Loc, at the back, who had the more difficult job though since his steering controlled *Day Bringer*'s approach to bends and bridges. Marheh could not even help by taking the tiller. She looked up at Kel.

"I think I shall go into my cabin and sulk."

He laughed at her.

"That would be a waste of a nice morning."

"They're doing very well aren't they?"

He nodded.

"Why don't we go and sit in the well deck and relax?"

"We should go and smile at Loc," she said. "But the well deck might be a bit ... public... for relaxing."

She watched his face. He wasn't smiling with his mouth but his eyes danced.

"Just what are you suggesting?" he asked softly.

She looked down demurely then raised large, innocent eyes to his.

"Nothing really," she said.

* * * *

They reached the turning place about an hour and a half after leaving Clanning. Gelis and Loc had been very careful and the journey had taken longer than it would normally have done. They took *Day Bringer* a little beyond it and moored up. The next move would be up to Marheh.

The two apprentices met on the tow path after carefully securing the two Yareblis boats.

"I wonder what will happen to them," Gelis said. "Are there any Yareblis left to use them?"

Loc shook his head.

"Probably not in Clanning, not after what Marheh did, but maybe somewhere else."

"They've been very quiet," Gelis said, indicating towards *Day Bringer*.

"I wouldn't be surprised if they've both been asleep," Loc said. "The work they did in Clanning will have taken a lot out of them."

"They really care about each other, don't they?" Gelis said carefully.

"Yes, they do," Loc said. "They've been soul friends, committed to each other, for more than thirty years and they've known each other since Marheh was apprenticed, which must be fifty years ago."

"But they've never married."

Gelis sounded a bit wistful.

"Silberay don't," Loc said. "You know that. How could we and still do the work we train for?"

"I suppose so. I mean, I do understand, but… you must have seen the way they look at each other sometimes. Why can't they be together?"

"They are together," Loc said. "They practise the discipline of the mind with each other as well as singing together. They couldn't be more intimate than that and if, on the infrequent occasions when they are in the same place, they choose to be together in any other way, well, it's their own business. They're both mentors, they've the right to decide now."

Gelis flushed.

"I didn't mean to be nosy. I care about Marheh so much."

Loc nodded.

"I know that. You'll understand better when you are more practised at the disciplines."

They strolled along the tow path together, enjoying the sunshine.

"Marheh keeps apologising because we haven't had much practice, but there really hasn't been time, not with everything that's been happening," Gelis said.

"Things should be quieter for a while now," Loc said. "Marheh will make you work."

"That's what I want."

They wandered quite a way, turning occasionally to check the boats for any sign of activity. There was a bridge not far ahead and without needing to confer they climbed to the top of the arch and stood leaning on the brick balustrade looking back along the water road. Clanning was just a smudge on the horizon and the landscape around them was not particularly inspiring but it was quiet and peaceful, restful after the stressful time they had experienced in the last few weeks. They stood for a while in quiet contemplation until a figure emerged on *Day Bringer*'s back deck.

"Time to go back," Gelis said.

She smiled at Loc.

"I wonder what will be next."

* * * *

Next, it seemed, was a light meal, followed by time to plan.

"*Day Bringer* will go back to Deerford," Marheh said firmly. "We need to tell the people guarding the bridge and the tunnel that their job is complete and I need to pick up the new clothes Fali promised to make for me. It's time I stopped wandering about in my dressing gown because I haven't any dry trousers."

She turned to look at Gelis with mock severity.

"And I need to do some serious work with my apprentice, can't have her slacking off."

Gelis grinned.

"No, Ma'am."

"Obviously we'll need to travel with you back to *Storm Cloud*," Kel said. "But I'm wondering whether we should check in at the Harbour and keep Yarla in touch with what has happened."

Marheh nodded.

"I wonder whether any of the others have made their way there. They would not all have needed to stay in Deerford once their boats were cleaned up and they had recovered from their imprisonment."

"Were there any decisions made about routes at the Gathering, do you know?"

Marheh shook her head.

"There couldn't be. I'm sure Yarla had some ideas but so few boats made it to the Gathering that nothing could be decided."

"Except to send you to the rescue," Loc said.

Marheh raised her eyebrows and shrugged.

"I was the obvious choice." She smiled at Gelis. "And my poor apprentice just had to go along with it."

Kel stood up.

"We might as well get these dishes out of the way and get going. There's no need to hurry whatever we decide, but I would like to get back to *Storm Cloud* and make sure she is alright."

Marheh nodded. She understood his concern. *Storm Cloud*, the boat he lived on with his apprentice, had been left behind when they picked up the Yareblis boats for their approach to Clanning.

"Do you want to take one of the Yareblis boats and go ahead with Loc?" she asked. "They don't create as much wash as *Day Bringer*. You could go a bit faster."

He took plates from the table and went to the galley. Loc and Gelis jumped up to help.

"I think we will need one of the Yareblis boats for sleeping on anyway," he said. "But no need to go ahead, an extra day won't matter."

He came back towards her and she heard him in her mind. "I don't want to leave you yet."

She sent him a moment of warmth then stood up.

"I am going to turn *Day Bringer*," she declared. "By myself."

She put her chin in the air.

"You can go out on the bank and jeer when I mess it up or just lounge around in here."

Kel laughed.

"Oh, we'll go and jeer, won't we?"

He looked at the two apprentices.

"Jeering it is," Loc said.

Gelis said nothing and Marheh thought she looked a little worried. She smiled at her.

"Of course I'll do it beautifully, so jeering won't be necessary."

"Says you," Kel teased.

She gave him her best Marheh the Great look.

"I'll let you finish the dishes while I do the engine checks."

She took extra care over these, since *Day Bringer*'s engine had been silent for longer than usual. It felt good to be doing something so ordinary after the events of the last week or so. The engine started smoothly and she stood on the back deck listening to it for a few moments before stepping off to tackle the mooring lines. The other three were sitting on the ground beside the tow path.

"Jeer, jeer," Kel said as she passed them.

She put her tongue out at him.

The lines were quickly dealt with and then she was at the tiller gently engaging the throttle and nosing *Day Bringer* forward into the turning place. It felt as if her world had righted itself and she forgot about the watchers on the bank. *Day Bringer* was alive again.

The turning place was only just long enough to accommodate her *Boat* And she took special care to centre the bow exactly before

189

beginning to pivot. The stern moved smoothly around until it was again in the channel of the water road. A bit of reverse eased the bow out of the turning place and a minute or two later *Day Bringer* was pointing away from Clanning on her new course.

She acknowledged a bit of derisive cheering from the bank with a small bow. It was tempting to keep going but instead she slotted *Day Bringer* perfectly into place between the two Yareblis boats, moored up neatly and efficiently and turned off the engine.

"Show off," Kel said coming towards her. "Now what?"

"Now we sing," she said firmly.

That was the real healing, she thought afterwards. The song had washed through her carrying away the pain of all that had happened in Clanning. It had helped her to come to terms with what she knew to be Jik's death too. He had given her all he had left of life when her need was desperate. That extra strength had been enough to save her and enable her to finish the work she had undertaken in Clanning. He had been ninety six. She had known when she left the Harbour after the Gathering that she may not see him again. Her Silberay uncle had been a special part of her life for as long as she could remember and she would mourn his passing, but not the way of it. It had been a triumphant death and the way he would have chosen to go.

"Thank you Jik," she said quietly. "I'll try not to waste what you have given me."

She had been lying on her bed while she sang. Now she sighed and stretched and sat up to study her surroundings. It had been such a short time since the Gathering, weeks rather than months, and so much had happened. She was aware that she had not really made this cabin her own. The back cabin that now belonged to Gelis still felt like home to her. Now was the time to change that. She had to let go of the past and make space for her apprentice.

She stood up and opened the doors to the well deck. As she got older Nemle had like to lie in bed and watch the world go by. It was hard to imagine herself as old as that but letting the outside in had always been important.

For a few minutes she stood by the doors looking out. She had made a commitment to her apprentice at the Gathering and she was doing her best to honour it. She straightened and turned. Now it was time to make a commitment to the future. It would still hold work and challenge, but it had also to hold love and the relinquishing of self. These must accompany her now until the end of her life if she was to honour Jik's gift and Nemle's teaching and example.

"I promise," she said aloud, and made her way through to the galley to put the kettle on.

ABOUT THE AUTHOR

Rosalind, like many Australians, loves to travel. She fell in love with the canals of England during her first visit there and this has remained a life-long passion. She spent nearly three years living and traveling aboard a 37ft narrow*Boat A*nd this experience has informed her writing so that although the stories are fantasy the boating experience is authentic.

When not writing she enjoys walking her dog, practicing her violin, painting watercolours, choral singing, reading and of course traveling.

Marheh can be contacted at Marheh@gmail.com

Or keep up to date with Rosalind's writing at
https://rosalindkentwell.net/

www.ingramcontent.com/pod-product-compliance
Lightning Source LLC
Chambersburg PA
CBHW021147130626
46554CB00005B/1707